THE COAST OF MALABAR

THE COAST OF MALABAR

John Maher

THE O'BRIEN PRESS
DUBLIN

First published 1988 by The O'Brien Press Ltd.
20 Victoria Road, Rathgar, Dublin 6, Ireland.

British Library Cataloguing in Publication Data
Maher, John
The coast of Malabar
I. Title
823'.914[F]

ISBN 0-86278-166-3

Typesetting: The O'Brien Press, 10/13 Schoolbook
Book design: Michael O'Brien
Printing: The Guernsey Press Co. Ltd., Guernsey, Channel Islands

The publisher acknowledges the assistance of
The Arts Council/An Chomhairle Ealaíon
in the publication of this book.

Contents

For Mai and Shem

The Coast of Malabar

HE SITS GAP-TOOTHED AND GRINNING. Eyes upon all about him. Lips tainted with bitter retorts. An old man now, John. Seedless belly. Short measure dealt for all. He grins again, then angles himself before his circle of listeners. Like a death's head beckoning in malice. Smiling, his listeners crowd about him. They hear John tell again the tale of the man, the woman and the sojourner.

—Dillon and her. There he is now. Over in the corner. Well, speak of the devil! They both shacked up together in a small flat off the Broadway. Oh, they were like that for a few years. All grand and easy. Before she took ill, that was.

It is morning. They wake as one. Dull light of a winter's morning tilting at their senses once more. Dillon lays his hand upon her head. They speak softly over breakfast, then part. He drives off to his employment bureau. A taskmaster. Days spent talking with those who are passing through. Short-term jobs. She, Ann, takes the train to a Polytech. Colours on cloth. Waxed images. In the evenings they meet again. They seldom go out at night. They sit and read. They talk. She sketches. Sometimes the phone rings. Dillon is brief and direct when he speaks to the unseen voices. At times, lifting his head from the 'paper, he watches her as she walks towards the kitchen or turns to fetch something. He wonders how it would feel to have her presence taken away from him. He damns the notion as soon as he notes its pull.

The listeners take their ease a moment. The older man, John, puts his hand into his pocket. He calls for another round. He picks at his teeth with a matchstick. Winks towards his audience. Someone nods at him. At John. Old sag-bellied teller of tales. Quietly begrudging of the lives about him. He will talk on about the man, the woman and the stranger. The others listen, smiling his careful smile.

—Whatever it was, she came down very sudden with it. Galloping consumption. Nice name for the other, I suppose. You'd never be told anyway. He tried to nurse her himself, you see. Spent half the day looking after her. Neglected the business of course. Spent every penny he had on the best treatment available. That was the sort of him. Anyway, she was past help. She was already gone too far by the time the illness was discovered. Do you follow me?

It is morning. Dillon hears her as she tries to stifle a cough. He returns to the bedroom in haste. She fixes her gaze upon the book in her hands. Sitting on the edge of the bed, he lays his hand upon her head.

—I can stay for the day. It's no problem.

—No, you won't. It's alright again now.

—Are you sure?

Alone, he wanders about the kitchen, affecting to tidy things away. He delays in order to hear if she will cough again. He wonders now at what will happen to him when her presence is drawn away. A coldness comes upon his thoughts.

John, grown goutish and arrogant in his years. The listeners disperse for a moment, to watch a tall man pot a pool ball. They return again. He gathers them about him, waiting until they have all been baited by his silence. Then he leans forward once more. The callous grin of the careful storyteller. He beckons to them. The white shirt, the stout frame. A bloated smile. John tells on, of the man, of the woman and of the stranger.

—Just after Christmas it was. The worst time of the year you could pick. She went very quickly. Don't ask me whether she was in pain or not. I suppose they had her on some kind of dope towards the end. Brompton cocktail. Isn't that what they call it? He lost his reason. Before she was even buried. We used to see him in here. He took it very bad. Broke up completely, he was. Became very hard in himself. Wouldn't speak to anyone. Hadn't a civil word for his own friends even. He stayed that way for a long time. He went back home for the funeral, you see. That was a real mistake. To set foot back home at all. Why couldn't he leave well enough alone? A very thick-headed man, Dillon.

Rains cutting in swathes across a grey churchyard. Dillon stands at a distance from the dead girl's family. Red-cheeked mother by the gaping grave. Salt spray on wind-blushed skin. The father. Thin reed of a soft-tempered man. His sons and daughters refusing, as one, to glance back towards the intruder standing silently by the stile. This was all then: a train journey back to Dublin after the funeral. A boat back across the sea. Then, the first evening alone in the apartment. Sitting, crying in his cups. Falling to sleep without relief. The evenings without number after that. Sounds coming from other rooms. He would turn, startled, then read her absence once again in the bitter silence. Slowly, the heart hardening as the months passed. Drifting back to that out of which he had so recently come. Emigrants in gloomy pubs. Their weekend haunts. Brash talk and heavy drinking. The coldness of his words telling those who knew him of the dying of the heart.

Hang-jowl John, eager now to continue the tale, carries on. The listeners, half-dozing before his words. Of the woman who died, of the man. Of the stranger who called one day. He moves his chair in towards the table. Elbow on the damp surface. Jabs with his finger. He calls his hearers closer. Gap-toothed smile to damn all about him.

—He turned in on himself after that. Then he went wild again. He'd be out 'til all hours of the night. Big red eyes on him. You'd see him in here often—over there in the corner by the phone. He'd be sitting there, as true as Jesus, chatting away to himself. Nobody paying a blind bit of attention to him at all. A thing which went against his business in the end. I believe he became so crooked in himself that he went and gave some big donation to some sort or political appeal or other. They saw him coming. I think, myself, that he would have lashed out at anybody in the state he was in at the time. It all seemed to come to a halt a short while after this chap turned up on his doorstep. Looking for a start he was. Anywhere. A stranger. Took Dillon out of himself a bit. Gave him somebody to worry about besides himself. And he did his best for the chap. Fed him and clothed him too, from what I hear. Sorted him out with a soft number up in Harlesden. There are three sorts they say you should never begrudge your company to. A widow, a blind man and a stranger. A bird of passage. And that's what the chap was. Only a bird of passage. But Dillon didn't see that. Or maybe he didn't want to see that. Sure he almost adopted the chap. More fool he.

Dillon sits in his office. There is a young man before him. A stranger, with a quiet and watchful manner about him. Dillon sees a young man, soft-tongued and straight from the boat. The stranger sees a middle-aged man, strangely uneasy for his years. After sorting out an interview for the stranger, Dillon stands up to put on his coat. He taps his watch.

—I want you back here by eleven tomorrow. Right?

—I'll be here on the dot.

—Where did you get my name from, if it's no harm to ask?

—Below in the Cock. Last night.

—Steer clear of that kip, will you. Rough lot. All talk merchants.

—I will.

—Eleven tomorrow, horse. For the cards and the rest of it. Good luck.

The following morning, having arranged for registration with a friend at the exchange, Dillon drives the young man back to his own flat. He gives him a clean shirt to wear for the interview. They sit together over coffee. The younger man looks about the flat. Bookcases. Potted plants, ceramics. Prints. Kandinsky. Batiks. Dillon notes the eyes which measure all.

—I live here on my own. Since my girlfriend died.

—Oh ...

—Most of that stuff up there belonged to her. Prints. That kind of thing. I wouldn't bother my arse throwing it out.

—I know what you mean.

He drops the young man by the tube station, allowing him find his own way to the interview. Then he turns back for the bureau once more.

Someone has taken the stage. He sits before the piano. It is evening now. John gives grudging ear to the songs. Sometimes he talks over the music, drawing his company away from the familiar words and the melodies well-worn. The number about him has dwindled to a pair of young labourers and a stray who had chanced in with them. Dillon has taken a seat at the next table. John, his tongue idling a moment, turns his back on the rough-haired man at the piano who sings an odd, jaunty Cockney song.

—Where was it I was? Ah, yes. Well, anyway, he took the young lad in. Bed, board and all. It was the company he was after, you see. A funny thing that, you might say. To take a complete stranger in under your roof. Never mind if it was one of your own. They spent a lot of time together too. They used go out to things. He stopped chasing his tail around the pubs, anyway. The young lad got a chance to find his feet over here. It was six of one. There was nothing unnatural about the business, if you see what I'm driving at. They were just company for one another. That was all.

It is evening. Rain bears down upon the city outside. Dillon sits by the dull light of the table lamp, scouring the morning paper. In the kitchen, the young man sits writing a letter. There is a print hanging on the wall behind him; a man leaning over a gate, watching the progress of the seasons. Smiling, a dark man. Autumn in one corner of the field; spring at the opposite end. In the gap between, the callous sun of high summer giving onto the cold, cramped earth of winter. Dillon calls from his newspaper. Later on, they drive down to the Broadway and take the late hour in a noisy bar. They have spoken at length over the months. The younger man has learned to listen without question as he sips at his drink. Dillon speaks of the woman's decline. The younger man listens, bearing the undertones of bitterness with patience. Slowly, Dillon comes around to mentioning her by name. Uneasily, at first, he tags tales onto his memories of her. When he plays cards, he sometimes looks away from his companions as her name starts to drift across his tongue. Then, one day as they sit together at evening, he speaks his sadness to the younger man.

—Is it worth all the trouble? Never again, boy. No, James. Never again. I couldn't take it twice.

The singer steps down from the podium to take a rest. The crowded bar falls back into smaller groups again. John, sag-bellied and saw-toothed, leans across the table towards the two labourers. The man at the next table does not hear. He is lost to those about him. He muses to himself as one in pursuit of some secret melody. John hunches up his shoulders and, glancing at the silent one at the next table, continues. His lips are set in an attitude both of distaste and mockery. He rubs his stubbled chin and winks at the two labourers. He snaps his fingers.

—And then, just like that, the young chap is gone again. Not a trace. Just when Dillon was starting to pull himself together. There's gratitude for you. He fed him, he clothed him. And the young chap goes and does a moonlight without as much as a word of thanks. The little get! And what did Dillon think of it all? Will you riddle me that, says the fellow. Anyway, I heard a long time after, that the cute little bollox had took off back home with some quare one. There's love for you. Love you and leave you!

It is a cold, damp morning and an evil sky sits over the city. Dillon stumbles from his bedroom and calls the young man for work. There is no answer. He calls again, then knocks slowly on the bedroom door. There is no-one within. Turning on the light in the kitchen, he sees the note lying on the table. He recognises the handwriting, but will not read the message. He casts the milk bottle he holds onto the cold, tiled floor. When he finally leaves the flat for the office, he will take his humour from the sky above and his comfort from the misery of those about him.

They are calling out his name now.
—John! John! Give us a bar of a song there!
Gap-toothed, he smiles at their number. The two labourers bang their pint glasses off the table. To one side the dark man, Dillon, watches as John in his frayed suit ascends the stage. Through eyes heavy with the evening's drink. He leans back in his chair as the labourers quit their clamouring. John looks down from the podium.
—Alright. I'll give ye one so. You won't be able to say I wouldn't oblige. A sad one. I like the sad ones best. I think you have probably all heard me sing it before now.
He clears his throat and glances back towards the piano.

—Far away across the ocean
Underneath an Indian star
Dwelt a lovely dark-eyed maiden
On the coast of Malabar.

The pianist moves his hand over the keys. Slowly, he threads the sullen tune onto the words he hears. Dillon shifts in his chair and looks up at the figure on the podium. Words threading thoughts threading words. When first I foot set in this city. Rooming houses and sweat of man. Men who must spend the rest of their days before the shovel. Then leaving these behind for an office. To mix with the sort who worked the men who worked the shovel. An office and a name. Two rooms on the Broadway. Girl typing in the next room. An apartment. And you, soft Ann. And why, then, suddenly this?

—She would raise her lovely dark eyes
And point across the bay
And whisper, 'If you love me
Why do you sail away?'

John, swaying as he sings. Someone at the bar turns back to his drink. The two labourers at the next table watch Dillon. They see his eyes drift from sense and sound.

A cry once, he, Dillon, heard. On the bare night, once. Room in a big house. Storm over Kilburn. Chinese girl. Keening to herself and wailing the whole night through. Soul-lost sound. Hearing the following morning that her child had died the previous day. Like print on the wall in the flat. Ann's print. James who explained it first. Walked by it a thousand times and never looked. Four panels, I think. Yes. In the corner, a skeleton dressed in top hat and tails with a big smirk on his puss. Watching the seasons pass in turn. Why did they take you? What did I not do?

> —I can see that crowded city
> With its palm trees green and tall
> And the starry night she danced with me
> Inside the city hall.

Someone calls from the crowd.
—Come on, John! Good man, Kearney!
The two labourers bang their glasses off the table. The singer looks down at Dillon. Eyes fixed on the floor. Glass held awkwardly in hand, set to fall. Lights dimming all about. Time! A bell ringing. All is gone, I know. A wife once, then a sort of son. You both. I will go no more to love you. And then, what is there? Him, smiling by the gate. This, there on the table. And you, John, up on the stage. I see you alright, you bull-nosed bastard. Smiling by the gate. Watching all the seasons pass. Never chance your crooked heart for anything. If it were to happen a thousand times again. Not like you I would be. A thousand times. Rather than you. A thousand times.

> —Fare thee well my lovely dark eyes
> Fare thee well my Indian star
> For I'll go no more and love you
> On the coast of Malabar.

The bell is ringing now and there are hands sounding applause. John, teller of the tale, gap-toothed and grinning, is smiling from the podium. Before him, the two labourers sit, sated with the story. One nods to the other and they call to the man at the microphone as they stand up to leave. And there is talk and chatter all around and words left unrequited in each ear. And there is the dark man, alone at his table. Memory stilled for another evening. Water settling once more over a chance pebble cast into a stagnant pool. Dillon, senseless by three empty chairs.

Gianni Mi Ha Ferita

ON THE CURTEST DAY OF THE YEAR, a weary sun struggled along the face of Hardwicke Place to the north of the river. A small boy with a strawberry birthmark on his left cheek ran whooping past the solemn shades of St George's Church and the hospital which flanked it. There, in a cramped room to the rear of Temple Street Hospital, Miriam Lehane turned quietly from the two social workers sitting across the table from her. The man beside her took her hand gently. As she drew her eyes to the floor once more, the taut, tetchy tones of the woman who had lived above them in their flat near the canal came stalking her memory once more.

—*Come here, my little damsel. Come here and see what Miss Hayes has in her pocket. Well!*

She heard the hospital's social worker, Miss Walthew, take up the thread of the tale now. But her eyes refused to counter those of the stout narrator before her, falling instead upon the symbols and portents of unease about the room. That photograph of the Mall, Westport, County Mayo, which stood over the sequence of the days of December. The clock on the wall behind the social workers which, by chance and the hour, happened to give the correct time. Miss Walthew was going over the details of the pending assault case for them once more. She inclined her head towards them as an earnest of intimacy. Once more the tale was told of a child hurt and of the questions which must be answered. Did they understand the gravity of the case at all? Miss Walthew doubted it. Mr McGettigan beside her, the health board's man, seconded her suspicions with a timely nod. Miriam Lehane glanced from the pair of telephones on the table to the folder which lay in front of Mr McGettigan. They could call him Tom. Both herself and John Callaghan beside her could call him Tom, if they liked. But they did not. Miss Walthew stabbed the air with her index finger. Her pouting chin seemed to burlesque the very words she spoke.

—The simple fact of the matter is, Miss Lehane, that we can take your child into care.

Outside on the corridor, an unnamed child screamed as it was carried into casualty. But no one in the room paid the sound any moment. Miss Walthew tugged at the lapels of her ochre blouse. Her words were without waste or ornament. The tiny petulant mouth sieved well what little emotion the eyes squandered. She placed her hands upon the table, palms upwards. The gesture seemed at once both odd and unsettling to the couple before her.

—And there you have it.

—And if I ... if we go to a solicitor?

Mr McGettigan was smiling uneasily at them now, as though to dull the blow which was coming. Beside her, Miriam Lehane felt her man's temper turn. She tried hard to keep her eyes upon the gaudy epaulettes of Mr McGettigan's jumper. Did he not realise that he was too old for such clothes? Miss Walthew turned towards her companion.

—A place-of-safety order. We won't even need you in court. Mr McGettigan here can confirm that.

—And you're telling us that Miriam here can do nothing about her own child. Is that the size of it?

There was the rasp of unrequited rage in the young man's voice now. And tears soused Miriam Lehane's eyes. For Callaghan beside her. For Callaghan with his long, herring-bone coat and his puzzled eyes who was fighting for her. Who was fighting for herself and her daughter. And they were to take the child from her now. And nothing else mattered. For something someone else had done. A cold, twisted spinster who had lived in the gloomy flat above them on Leeson Street. Miss Hayes, with her gentle grey hair. Operatic records on the air at evening. Miss Hayes, who hated low talk and drunkenness. She recalled sitting in the older woman's flat one evening. How Miss Hayes lost herself for a moment as she lilted that odd Italian song she was forever crooning. The child running about on the floor, pulling at this and that. The scarred plastic on the turntable between them. Gentle Miss Hayes, lilting to herself, tilting her head from one moment to the next to catch the swell in the soprano's voice at the end of each phrase. How did it go now?

—*Gianni mi ha amata.*

For every time the melody touched her now, the woman's face was before her eyes. The steady trill of the old lady's voice bearing the bruised melody back to memory. And the hatred in her heart for Miss Hayes, the author of all this unease. Why had Miss Hayes done that to her child? What illness was in her that had caused poor Emer to suffer so much? And why had she not realised what was going on in time?

But Miss Walthew had raised her voice now. And Callaghan was on his feet, jabbing his finger in accusation at the two social workers. And Mr McGettigan was fetching tissues for her. And she was crying. For the child would surely be taken from her now. And she was without words to tell her grief. What a random course her heart had run over the past week. A tired, merciless course between hatred and self-pity. Now, drained of any sense of the days passing, she sat before her inquisitors with nothing in her mind but the intolerable malice towards the woman who had instigated the whole torment. And where was she now?

—*Gianni mi ha ferita.*

Oh, how was it the melody went? When she sought it, of course, she could not find it. That was the way of things. What you wanted you never found. Yet it would waylay her when she least wished to hear it. And the words were so lovely too. But no! She must pay attention to what they were all saying around her. For it was important. She must not slip away again. They would accuse her once more of not taking the matter seriously. And Callaghan was swearing at them now. At Miss Walthew and Mr McGettigan. They would take her child away now. Little Emer with her lisp and smile. 1904 Children's Act.

Twenty-four hours. Words glancing off her, hurtling into the distance.

—If you would only let us finish. Please, Mr Callaghan.

—Give her a date, then. When will you leave the child back to her? When? When? Blast you! Blast the both of you!

John Callaghan's frantic, fearful eyes. Those wild sideburns which lent to his appearance that sharpness which was not native to his character. His face scored by a remorseless adolescence. Miscast in a parable not of his own making.

His hand, when it finally came down upon the desk in temper, drove both receivers from their cradles. And Mr McGettigan was standing now, clutching the file in his hand. But the middle-aged woman in the sensible tweed suit did not move from her chair and remained staring up into the eyes of the young man above her. Miss Walthew attended, with manifest patience, until a break in his protestations allowed her leave to speak with ease.

—The guards must prosecute, Mr Callaghan. It is out of your hands and it is out of our hands, I'm afraid.

Miriam Lehane almost had the words now. But wasn't Italian so musical though? Smooth, round forms. Like the women they sculpted. Not out of nature, of course. No hips for babies. Like her with Emer. Yes! That was how it went. They were all shouting around her now and still, through the veil of her tears, she heard the gentle voice come tugging at her senses once more.

—*Gianni mi ha amata*
Gianni mi ha ferita
Gianni mi ha amata
Ecco! Lo portano via.

About someone who murdered his lover. Miss Hayes had told her that much. And they took Gianni away. And good riddance of course, said Miss Hayes, half in earnest. Any man that would raise his hand to a lady. Miriam Lehane laughed through her distracted tears. Someone should hurt Miss Hayes. Smiling Miss Hayes. Camomile and attar of roses. Oh, she swore by them. And her mother swore by them. Now, wasn't that a thing? Somebody should really hurt Miss Evelyn Hayes very badly.

But Miss Walthew's words had prevailed now and the men had suddenly fallen silent around her. And Mr McGettigan was thumbing through a notebook for telephone numbers. And Callaghan had lit a cigarette. And all she could think of was her child and that other song, that dark song Miss Hayes had taught little Emer lisping in the corner.

—Tramp, tramp, tramp the boys are marching

They were to return to the hospital in an hour's time. Miss Walthew and Mr McGettigan must consult on the matter in private and with higher authorities on the health board.

—Here come bobbies at the door

There was a café not too far away, Mr McGettigan said kindly. Sausage rolls and that kind of thing.

—If you do not let them in

Did Miss Lehane eat sausage rolls actually? Some people wouldn't touch them. He knew that for a fact.

—They will burst the door down

Miss Walthew opened the door for them. Mr McGettigan smiled, showing teeth stained with tobacco residues. The remnant of a cigarette rolled in liquorice paper lay in an ashtray on the desk.

—And you'll never see your daddy anymore.

Miss Walthew closed the door behind them. From the corridor, they heard her drag her chair closer to the desk as she spoke to her companion.

—Well, Tom, and where does that leave us?

As the young man and woman emerged from the laneway on to Temple Street, they heard a distant bell break the hour of noon. In the stark sunlight and without a word, they turned quickly for North Frederick Street.

In the café on the corner of Parnell Square, they spoke together. There might be, they had been told, the possibility of effecting some sort of compromise. If an understanding could be reached with the Midland Health Board, the child might be released into the custody of its maternal grandparents. There would have to be a series of consultations by 'phone. They must return to the hospital in an hour's time to discuss the matter afresh. At first, unnerved by the intensity of the debate in the hospital they felt unable to speak easily with one another. When Callaghan laid his hand on hers, Miriam Lehane shuddered at his touch. The young girl clearing away the adjoining table spoke to them casually. It was good to be in out of the cold. Was there anything in the morning paper about the expected boat strike? The accent was that of the girls with whom she herself had worked during her pregnancy. The blunt, dental sounds of the city's working classes. As she sipped the bitter, lukewarm coffee, Miriam Lehane was drawn back to the months before the birth of her daughter and the time she had passed with the child's father, Robert Darcy.

* * *

That autumn, she had arrived back from Longford to the boarding school on St Stephen's Green with an unusually light heart. She felt content, for once, to be back in the city. It refreshed her to savour once more the subdued chaos of the place. It became her custom, on half-days, to stroll down into the city with one of the day-girls. One afternoon, for fun, they wandered into a pool hall on the quays. Where the unemployed and semi-employed of the city passed their free hours and made contact with one another. The air was thick with their shouts and curses. Lean figures with cue-sticks, calling out to one another in the half-dark. She was standing in his path when Robert Darcy stumbled into her as he rounded a table. They chatted to one another during the game. The following week, she sought him out on her own. The world in which he moved and into which she was subsequently drawn, bore little resemblance to the city as she perceived it from St Stephen's Green. Darcy dealt in a number of markets around the town. The words he used to shackle the realities of his life constantly confounded her. They began to see one another more often. Sometimes they would meet,

21

on her free afternoons, in a pub down by the Four Courts. Shortly after Christmas she took to passing, with written permission, every odd-weekend with the family of a day-girl from the North Strand. On these occasions, she would spend most of her time with Darcy, returning to her friend's house in the early hours of the morning. By the time Easter arrived, and she had begun to worry about her exams, she discovered that she was bearing a child. The reaction of her own family was unhelpful. Her mother sat in a brutal silence in the corner of the room, while her eldest sister tried to console her. Her father, while admonishing her for her behaviour, suggested that she stay at home and take her exams the following year after the birth of the child. Walking down by the barracks in Longford that evening, she resolved to return to Dublin, to ignore both school and exams and to set herself up with a flat and a job.

*   *   *

Callaghan reached across the table to take her hand, almost upsetting her coffee as he did so.

—They will give her back to you, Miriam, I'm sure of it.

—How?

—Well, they wouldn't be going to all that trouble 'phoning around otherwise. Would they?

—I don't know. I don't know what to think.

*   *   *

Heavy with her child, she arrived back in Dublin after the Easter break and was surprised to find that the only job she could obtain was in a cake shop. In a Kylemore near O'Connell Street, she passed the days before the birth wrapping bread and boxing cakes. There were conversations with the other shopgirls about men and money. They were all considerate towards her. One of them, a tall gangling girl from one of the great nameless estates to the north of the river, came back with her to her bedsitter in Rathmines one evening. Miriam was astonished to find that the girl appeared lost in that quarter of the city. She was even more disappointed to discover when they had settled down after dinner, that they had nothing whatsoever to say to one another. It was a revelation to her, that the strange words her companion used betokened not merely another manner of speaking of the world, but the existence of another world itself. Over the hot scourge of that summer — the first days were punctuated by the assassination of the British ambassador — she spent most of her free time in the company of Robert Darcy. He appeared ill-at-ease with the idea of moving into the bedsitter and contented himself with passing the weekends there. She assumed that, after the birth of the child, matters would be different. Already, there was talk of approaching the Corporation for some form of accommodation. Meanwhile, Robert Darcy remained in the flat he shared with his mother and two sisters, off Dorset Street.

* * *

—*I just want to touch you. Mine that I lost. Does your mammy not love you? I will look after you. Little woman of mine. The beautiful hair you have. Your little smile. Like her, you are, Emer. Ah, Jesus, why do they take you from us? I will mind you now until she comes home. Let me hold you tight. No! No! I didn't mean to hurt you! Ah, why are you crying, child of grace?*

* * *

Throughout the summer of her burden, she went all over the city with Darcy. Sometimes she would even go down with him in the van on the Sunday mornings to help with the dealing in the Cumberland Market. Accordingly, she acquired a good knowledge of the city and the set of its working-class suburbs. On one occasion, she went with Darcy to a house out in Ballyfermot, after the funeral of one of his uncles. The drinking and the arguments, with the corpse scarcely in the ground, appalled her. She recalled the arrival of the other uncles, who lived around the Gloucester Diamond. Their heavy bearing and buckled belts made her uneasy. Darcy whispering to her that they were only animals. One of them smiled over at her from the doorway. Darcy's mother kept her near to her throughout the evening, as though trying to protect her from her new family. In such a fashion, she became acquainted with Darcy's extended family, his close friends and the underculture from which they had emerged. She understood that her child's father was settled at his own level in the world and that he had security of tenure there. She was also aware that she had not far to fall to join him. A short while after the birth of the baby, she moved with Darcy into a Corporation flat in Marrowbone Lane, which was occupied by Darcy's grandmother. From there it would be possible, on grounds of overcrowding, to secure a flat for themselves within a short time.

*　　*　　*

Callaghan was whispering now. His hands were palm-to-palm, as if in an attitude of mock prayer.

—How were we to know what was going on, Miriam?

—We should have known. With the marks and all.

—And what could we have done?

—Asked somebody. You know plenty of people.

—Look, there's no point in blaming yourself, Miriam. If someone had told you that a babysitter would do this ... another woman ...

—What does it matter, whether it was a woman or a man?

—Would you have expected a woman?

—I just don't know. I just know that I would put a knife in her right now, so I would. And I wouldn't care.

—That'll get us nowhere.

—And would you be so cool, if it was your child it was? Would you?

—That's not fair.

—No ... I'm sorry. I don't suppose it is.

—Come on. Let's be getting back.

They were appearing in for lunches now. Workers from the council offices and others. The windows of the small café began to mist themselves against the cold noon air.

As the first glut of office workers settled about the table opposite them, they rose to return to the hospital. Along Gardiner Row they walked, killing the hour by the time they had reached Belvedere. A couple hurried past them along the laneway beside the hospital. The man bore in his arms a young girl wrapped in a tartan blanket. They could hear the woman's voice echoing along the corridors as they entered the building. Outside the office, Miriam doused her cigarette. She turned to Callaghan to be held. He shook her gently, chiding her for her lack of faith.

—What will happen if they decide not to give her back?

—I don't honestly see that happening.

—You don't know.

—Alright. If they do ... if they do ...

—What?

—We'll do a runner. Over the border. With Emer. Make a big thing of it. With the papers.

—That's talk. All talk.

—Once the papers get hold of it ...

They knocked on the frosted glass and entered. It was explained to them that there had been consultations with the Midland Health Board. An arrangement might be reached. Should the child's grandparents be willing to accept temporary custody of the child, the local health board would agree to second one of its workers to the case. The child must be brought to Longford that evening however. And she must remain in the care of her grandparents until such time as both health boards decided otherwise. The implications of the decision were stressed by Mr McGettigan. Any attempt, he noted, to remove the child from the town of Longford, would be answered with a place-of-safety order. Allusions were made to decisions made in the past which the health boards had later found reason to regret. Children had suffered and the health board must protect itself from all accusations of laxity or lack of vigilance.

—For better or for worse, we are *in loco parentiis*. We cannot afford to take undue risks.

A woman appeared at the door bearing a tray and Miss Walthew called for an extra couple of cups. They spoke more freely now of the background to the whole affair. Of how the child had been on an access visit that particular weekend. It was Darcy's mother who had first noticed the marks on the child's buttocks and back when she came to undress her. The following morning, without informing her son, she brought the girl to a private doctor. The child was admitted to hospital on the strength of a single phone-call. The matter was to be treated, until further notice, as a case of suspected assault. Miriam Lehane found herself unable to recall much about that Saturday. There was Darcy's mother 'phoning her in the flat in Leeson Street. That was the only clear detail left to memory. The rest was a blurred composite of a taximan's smile and a traffic jam caused by a demonstration in O'Connell Street. At first, she could not fathom the true nature of the situation at all. Then, sitting with the child on her knee in the hospital ward, she came to understand that her daughter was no longer solely her concern anymore. Now that the health board had expressed its interest in the child's welfare, there was a fresh veto on any decision she might make. She brought the child over to the window and they pointed out the cars and the passers-by. The words tumbling from the child's lips, the one after the other. The message in the child's words threw her. The image of the woman in the flat above them. The coiffed hair, the small talk of weather and the world. The head nodding, the eyes watching.

—*Ah, little thing. I would look after you so well. More than that one. She doesn't deserve you. But I can't say that, can I? You are with me again for a little while only. That is all. Now, don't cry. Don't cry, child. There is no call to be afraid. Tighter I will hold you, little Emer. They will never take you away from me. Little love.*

She had lost Miss Walthew's voice for a moment, but now it came to her again. Clear, unequivocating tones clarifying the matter of their earlier discussion. She told them that both herself and Mr McGettigan had been astounded by their seemingly casual attitude to the whole affair. Perhaps they had not taken full account of the implications at the time? As she spoke, Miss Walthew turned for support to the man beside her. It had been necessary to draw them to a fuller realisation of the seriousness of the affair. Mr McGettigan ran a dampened finger along the liquorice paper in the palm of his right hand.

—We had to see what your reaction would be.

—I don't understand. Do you mean that you led myself and Miriam along just to get a rise out of us? Is that it?

Miriam Lehane, after the fashion of her father, bit her lower lip and thought of elsewhere. She tugged at her shoulder-length hair in the manner of the bewildered. Should she be crying now? She glanced about her for a cue. If only she had been listening.

—It wasn't a test, Mr Callaghan. We just thought you both needed to come out of yourselves ... to see the seriousness of the whole business.

What would her daughter have been thinking then? Breath, hands pressing down on her, woman, not mother, not mine. Child's pain and fright. But she should not even try to imagine it. And the awful mustard-coloured bruises which came up on the child's skin in the hospital. And how her daughter had cried when she lifted her from the cot and took her on her knee. That was the worst part of all — the rejection in the child's eyes, the utter despondency which stole its way into her own heart.

—A child's welfare has been put in jeopardy, Miss Lehane. Through negligence, ignorance or call it what you will. And the whole thing has been a shock for you. And, perhaps that's not a bad thing. And your daughter has been through quite a lot. I would like you to remember that.

—And what was the need of all this ... of all this ...

—Yes, Mr Callaghan?

Miss Walthew smiled without forethought as she lifted the receiver.

*   *   *

Miriam Lehane recalled for herself as she sat in silence, how the differences with Robert Darcy had first started in his grandmother's flat in Marrowbone Lane. She had found the new world hard to reason with. By day there was the sight of children running wild around the flats; by night, the sound of nameless cries and of bottles breaking. Darcy's grandmother Annie was easy enough to get on with. She bore the new imposition with the sort of fortitude which had seen her through the rearing of her own eight children. Some mornings, the old woman would take the child while she wandered off into the city for a break. It was on one of those days, when the child was almost a year old, that Miriam Lehane began to see the irrelevance of her relationship with Darcy. For months now they had spoken of greater things but little. Although they were afforded the chance of getting out quite often they found that, alone together, they had little left to say to one another. After a while, the arguments began to subside into an unfeeling coldness which might last a whole day. She recalled the morning Darcy had raised his hand to her and the words her lips bore. The mention of class and upbringing. And she thought now, as she sat facing the social workers, of the wrongness of her words. And how suspicion in the assault case relating to her daughter, had initially centred, because of his origins, on Darcy. But he had not struck her that morning, all the same. And Annie had remained in the kitchen calling out to them both in order to distract them. Then there was the aftermath of the argument. Tears by the fireside, while the child romped about on the floor. The old woman standing behind her, resting her hands on Miriam's shoulders. Her wizened face, the very seal of a hundred, hungry generations before her.

—It's hard for you, lovey, isn't it? When you're not with your own. I do see Robert there sometimes and, I declare to Christ, I don't know what does be in his head. My man was a bit like that too, you know. Rise a row like that, he would. We make them what they are, sure. Am I right, or am I wrong?

When they separated, Miriam moved with the child into a small bedsitter in Leeson Street. She went to work in a business equipment office on the quays and found a place for the child in the crêche. At first she accepted occasional maintenance money from Darcy. Then, as the bitterness between them increased with each meeting, she decided to refuse any further payments. She consented to access visits, however. On the first Friday of each month, Darcy would take the child to his mother's flat for the weekend. Waiting for the little red van to appear on certain Sunday evenings became an unnerving ritual. There was a vision she sometimes entertained, of Darcy sitting with her daughter on the deck of the mailboat as it pulled out to sea. Then, a council flat somewhere in London. And her daughter learning a new language once more. The tongue of the London-Irish worker.

In the house in Leeson Street, the child was drawn out of herself by the company of the other children in the flats about her. Her vocabulary began to encompass new ideas and she discarded many of the notions she had picked up in Marrowbone Lane. When John Callaghan, a civil servant, came into their lives, there were even greater changes. At first, the child made strange with her mother's visitor and spoke little in his company. Then, as the ache passed from her mother's eyes, the child became more trusting of the stranger. When Miriam finally consented to their living together, they moved to a larger flat in the basement of the house. With the change of abode, the child seemed to accept the change in status of the man who had come to live with them.

*   *   *

Miss Walthew rapped the table with her pencil as she spoke into the phone. Miriam Lehane could hear the earpiece beat out the tones of her mother's voice. Miss Walthew who weighed each word before she spoke.

—We have been given the option of allowing the child into your custody, should you be agreeable to that, or of keeping the child in care until the whole business with the guards has been sorted out. The health board feels that Emer's best interests would be served by returning her to a stable family environment. This would mean, of course, that she would have to stay in Longford until such time as the two health boards decided otherwise. Perhaps I might let you have a few words with your daughter, Mrs Lehane. She might be able to fill you in a little.

Then they were back in the ward again. The child must be brought down to Longford that evening. They could take the six o'clock train. Miriam could travel down each weekend from Dublin until such time as the investigation had been sorted out. As they emerged into the side lane, with the child running ahead of them, Miriam Lehane wondered at the hinterland of the heart, where the older bonds of parent and child lay. She thought of the household in Longford. Of her mother, slightly distant from her granddaughter. Of her father, indifferent to any hidden tensions in his affection for the child. Her older sister Helen would be there when they arrived in Longford that evening. Callaghan would get on well with her. Two public servants speaking with a shared arrogance of the world about them. They would have to find a new flat in Dublin right away. That much was clear. Callaghan could return to the city the next day and begin searching. Or perhaps they might stay in Longford over the Christmas? It was unthinkable that they might pass Miss Hayes on the stairs of the house in Leeson Street and know that she had not been brought to book yet for her misdemeanour. They had spent the past week in a friend's house and only needed to return once to move everything into a new flat. She pictured the woman's face as she tried again to gauge the turn of her thoughts.

—*Ah, little thing. They've taken you from me. All gone again. How I only wanted to hold you. That bitch! That whore! Liar is all she is! I never meant to hurt you. She knows that. Little Emer. I loved you. Like her, I did. They always take them away. Always.*

Her father was there to meet them from the Dublin train. The whole family were shocked by what they had heard. He pleaded softly with them not to let the matter go beyond the walls of the house. The shop windows along the main street and even the air of the evening seemed to tell that Christmas was less then a week off. They should stay in Longford over the holiday, her father offered. The child had fallen asleep by the time they reached the house on the Ballymahon Road. She was put down in a cot in the back room. At supper, the matter was turned over and over again. Her sister Helen poured tea but held herself aloof from the conversation.

The smells of the evening touched Miriam Lehane once more: the soda bread in the oven and memory of cloves threading the air from the baking earlier that day. After the meal, she helped her mother clear up. Her father took Callaghan and her sister down the town for a late drink. She sat in by the fire and tried to content herself with a magazine. It would take months to learn to live again, without feeling under emotional siege all the time. She could hear her mother humming to herself in the kitchen as the last of the dishes was dried and put away. The opening and closing of drawers. And, if the child chanced to have a fall and hurt herself and they got to hear about it, would they suspect her again? Her mother was sitting before her by the fire now. At first, they spoke in short bursts, touching upon the matter only distantly. Then, almost imperceptibly, they came to speak of the nature of the assault itself. Miriam told the tale again as bluntly as she might, fending off any questions which seemed too subtle of intent. They spoke of the woman in the lonely bedsitter in Leeson Street and speculated upon the impetus for her behaviour. Perhaps there had been some problem in the woman's past, her mother volunteered.

—There is always something there, you know. If you dig back far enough. It was the same when I worked in the County.

Her mother wondered why she had not suspected anything all along. Through the hindsight of the external narrator, the whole business seemed clear-cut enough.

Miriam Lehane was aware now that she should have taken the child's bruising more earnestly. Perhaps the recent arrival of Callaghan into their lives had caused her to neglect her duties. The bruising had first come to her attention after the bank holiday weekend. Wasn't that so? The morning after Miss Hayes had babysat the child. She quizzed herself, during her mother's intermittent silences, on the nature of her first impulse. Then, when her mother rose to put on the kettle, she was alone by the fire again. She left aside the magazine and took up the poker. Remorse and, in its wake an unknown grief, passed through her heart when she thought of her child in sleep.

—It's not much of a life, now. Is it, Miriam?

She felt disgust that she might have weighed her child's happiness against her own comfort. And she felt deeply mistrustful of herself now and wondered whether she would forever more.

—That's what myself and your father feel about it, anyway.

She wondered whether she was ill and whether her daughter should be taken from her. She was no longer sure that she had any rights to the child. In terror, she recounted that same query which had so troubled her in the days immediately following the child's hospitalisation. Could she herself have inflicted the injuries? Could some disorder or mental disaffection have helped her cloud the matter from memory? There could be no final telling, she acknowledged, save by the words of the woman from the flat above. Against the sound of her mother scalding the teapot in the kitchen, she felt only a numbness now and the pull of something urging her to flight.

—Would you not stay down here now and make a fresh start, lovey? Nobody need ever know.

Her mother left the tray down between them on a low table. Then she raised the lid of the teapot to give the dark liquid a final stir. Pouring with her left hand, keeping her eyes on the table before her.

—Are you alright, Miriam? You look very pale, girl.

—It's the other. I forgot about everything with the hospital and all.

—There's some aspirin up in the press, if you want it.

She could scarcely finish her cup. And her stomach was cramping again. She mounted the stairs to the bedroom. In the back room, the cot had been set beside her own bed. Leaning over the child and surprising her in sleep, she kissed her, promising that she would never again take a chance with her well-being. She opened the wardrobe quietly to find a nightdress. Her hand ran against one of her old gym-slips. Crimson. Loreto on the Green. Hours strolling about Dublin with her schoolfriends. A French teacher whom she had particularly admired. A joke too, she remembered. Perhaps she could try for her exams again. Was that silly, though? She felt older now than the sum of her hours, all of a sudden. She sat down on the bed and ran her hand over the crest on the blazer. The evening Darcy had coaxed her into wearing it in the flat in Marrowbone Lane. For a joke. How she had whispered to him to lower his voice so as not to waken the baby or disturb the old woman. The Coombe. Her mother and father standing in embarrassment by her bed while the shopgirls from the Kylemore passed the baby around. Her parents had never met Darcy either. She recalled the pain of labour and her initial astonishment at being a mother. And the young girl in the next bed, whom no man came to visit. She told herself that she would be different. There would be stability. Leaving the blazer in the wardrobe, she considered the new ways of living and the certainties her mother took for granted. It may be, she told herself, that there is a fresh path between the two women.

As her head turned to the pillow, she heard them return. Her father was telling a joke about some footballer on the county team. She heard her sister's laughter and her mother calling to them all to be quiet. Then, the mention of her own name and the sound of her mother making up the settee-bed for Callaghan. She checked the child once more, pulling down the blanket from her face. There was a thing that was on her mind, she told herself. There was something which had slipped by among her thoughts as she was being bundled towards sleep. An inkling, twisting and turning among the other notions. Then, breaking through the undergrowth of afterthought to confront her. It was a dark message, somewhere on the fringes of both remorse and hurt. That she would not dare name to herself in full waking. The face of her man before her, smiling in the half-dark. The thought that she might never again trust anyone with the child. And there was a chiller idea still, which she sought to drive away on impulse. For it could never have been he. Not with the time and the child's reactions and his manner. Could it? For all trust had been surely done down now. And this would prove the greater hurt, long after the other wounds had faded. She thought once more of the woman who had lived above them in the flat on Leeson Street. Of her ingratiating smile and of the severe order she kept in the tiny room. And she stretched out her hand once more, to stroke the child's forehead.

Weeping, she wondered at the tricks of the world and the days which lay ahead.

* * *

—*You are gone now, little thing. Away from me. Once, we were happy. They will be here again tomorrow, I suppose. Men in suits with questions and more questions. But I will not be here. Because I did not do anything. And what did that tramp say about me? What did she say about Miss Hayes? And why did they take you from me? Why do they always take you from me?*

* * *

But she did not curse the woman who had hurt the child for, had her mother not told her a thousand times that a curse might well find its way back to bind the maledictor?

Leah's Tale

THE CHILDREN HAD BEEN PUT to bed now and the evening was beginning to settle into night. The drawing-room was heavy with their silence. The older woman in the easy chair eyed her daughter-in-law by the window. She remarked to herself at the way Leah had of digging her hands into the pockets of her angora cardigan. This signalled stubbornness to her. Neither woman spoke. Leah kept her eye on the road outside and her back towards her mother-in-law. She was not a tall woman herself, but dressed to present the illusion of height. When she stood at the top of the steps to see her son off to the local school in Ranelagh, only the hands in the pockets of her cullottes concealed the tale of three children which her hips told. Her hair, drawn back from the high forehead she had inherited from her father's family, was tied in a pony-tail. When alone, she had the habit of chewing her hair before the mirror. She was a fair woman in most matters but would not tolerate cats in the home. In childhood, she had taught herself to remain silent when silence best served her purpose.

Both women could hear the student below in the basement flat in conversation with Robert, their words dulled by the distance between the two rooms. Leah noted how the garden had suddenly taken with the few days of sun. The cherry tree had come into bud again and the sharp light of the evening told spring and the turn of the seasons. She did not look around at her mother-in-law, but drawing on the cigarette, kept an ear for Robert's voice and his footsteps on the stairs leading up from the basement. Little Kate had been sick earlier that day and she felt that the child might be coming down with the virus which had been doing the rounds of the crèche. She wondered whether the child had sensed the fresh bitterness in the house that evening. Darragh had certainly suspected nothing. The boy had gone to bed almost as soon as he had been called in from the back garden and his games. For a moment, she took fright at the prospect of facing Robert. She was uncertain now for the first time as to how his temper might run. She would ask Robert's mother to leave the room when he came in, or else refuse to talk.

There were footsteps on the stairs and she drew hard on her cigarette. The woman in the easy chair coughed contentedly as she stretched across the coffee table to pick up the *Mail*. The woman seemed to be shivering as though a sudden chill had taken her. Leah recalled that Robert's mother always reacted in such a fashion when pressed by time or occasion. The woman in the chair stood up slowly. Leah's thoughts ran to the children once again. She thought of their eldest boy away at school in Glenstal. Of how he had changed since the previous summer. His disdain for Robert evident in each little comment made over the Christmas break. Her husband's sodden eyes at the festive table. The one day of the year. With quiet restraint, she drove the image from her as she had done a thousand times before. She took comfort in the knowledge that Robert would probably have been drinking earlier in the day.

—It can't go on like this, Leah. And Robert knows it too.
—I've said it to him.

Her mother-in-law folded the newspaper carefully as she made for the door. Leah turned to watch the woman and did not wonder at the joy she seemed to be taking in the distress. For Mrs John Palmer had no friends nor did anyone seek her company willingly. She had never pretended to like her daughter-in-law but had borne the imposition with a certain grudging grace. The walking-stick of flawed hazel in her hand was an affectation contrived to give an image of dignity and forbearance in old age. The brief conversations she had entertained with Leah over the years had never amounted to much. They had touched upon the bric-a-brac of living and no more. On the occasions on which she had spoken with Leah's mother, she had been secretly appalled by the memory of fields in Hattie Wilson's conversation. She approved neither of her daughter-in-law's rural origins nor of the trappings of a north Dublin childhood in her accent. Leah had a memory of the two women sitting before the fire in the drawing-room, her own mother scrambling to please with her answers while Robert's mother smiled the smile of a carefree inquisitor at ease in her own home. Hattie Wilson declared that she was happy with 'a cup of tea in her hand' and that she was 'fit to burst with all them cakes'. Mrs John Palmer lived on the memory of their encounters for weeks afterwards. Leah observed the studied pursing of her mother-in-law's lips, as she hummed to herself in a mocking exuberance. She wished that she could strike the woman. The tight grey curls, the dark sombre clothes. The choker she wore in defiance of her age. The masked tirades she had listened to so often. They always appeared to follow the self-same style. Her mother-in-law would begin by speaking of her late husband, of his diligence and good nature. She would tell of their time in Borneo together. Of the heat, the sickness and her fears for their own health and that of their child, Robert. She would speak of servants and tell a tale of flying to meet her husband in a strange city. Hiding in a grubby hotel with the child by her side. The filth of the sheets under which they had all slept. Then, her husband's malaria. How relations between them had been sullied by the recurring illness. There were phrases she would out with. Put to the pin of our collars, Leah. Life was such and had to be lived. Made the best of a bad lot. There was always the reference to the past when the problems of the present appeared. Like the thing Robert said to her years before, when he was courting her away from her studies.

—That's the way life works, Leah. Exposition, development, recapitulation. First movement form. With a little flourish or two. Isn't that it though?

—What's the point in living it at all if it's so predictable?

Robert dressed in sports jacket and open-necked shirt, waiting for her at the Traitors' Gate on Stephen's Green.

Around the time the North started. When was that? It seemed as if it had always been there.

The door opened and Leah turned away from the woman. She heard Robert enter the room and knew that her mother-in-law had left. From her position by the window, she could see a child cycling along the pavement in the direction of Ranelagh village. A couple sauntered by on the opposite pavement and she smiled at the prospect. She heard her husband close the door behind him and the footsteps of her mother-in-law on the stairs. She heard Kate cry in the bedroom and the woman on the stairs calling out to quieten her. She heard Robert's voice on the chilled air of the evening.

—I think we'd better have a talk, Leah. Just the two of us.

She turned to face the man by the door. The sallow complexion of the liver-ill was the most distinctive feature of his face. He crossed to the piano and slowly closed the lid as though to mute any possible distraction. His way of watching the world was that of a blackbird, she thought. The startled eyes, the peripheral vision of the neurotic. There was an intensity to his speech which showed him to be quite incapable of stillness. Across the room she heard him speak.

—What are we going to do, Leah?

She turned to face the man standing with his back to the mantelpiece. And she thought of the great stretch in the evenings now and of all that had happened in the past year.

So much had happened during the year. And so much at the one time. Edward had been preparing for Glenstal. Robert's mother was coming out of her winter cold and the bout of bronchitis to which she was subjected each spring. Robert himself had been involved with a new scheme. It had something to do with starting up an independent venture with someone in north Dublin. With someone he must have encountered on a morning session down around Capel Street and the early houses. The stocky little man became a regular visitor to their house for a time. Leah disliked his manner and the cute look in his eye. There were sessions late into the evening. There was great talk of undercutting and personal contacts with the growers out around Rush. Then, just as quickly, the scheme was abandoned. Had it not been for the deal which had been contrived before Robert's father died, they might well have had to abandon the family house long ago. When John Palmer noted that gentlemen no longer shopped for quality and goodwear, he sold his men's outfitters in Capel Street and bought into a vegetable business in the markets. He handed on his house and business interests to his only son on his death. There was to be no horseplay with death duties if at all possible, he had suggested. He left a sum in trust for his grandson's education and a separate sum for the comfort of his widow who must continue to reside in the family house. Robert Palmer took to the new venture in the markets with an enthusiasm which surprised himself. He no longer felt burdened by that talent he had displayed during his undergraduate years as a music student at Dublin University. He learned how to season the day's dealings with drink and within three years of his father's death had developed an alcohol dependency. In the fashion of the pubs he frequented, it was the common intelligence that he was working on something, the identity of which might only be hinted at in select company.

There were tales her husband had crafted for himself in various pubs around the city. A series of alter egos tailored to suit each individual audience in each particular drinking house. These disturbed visions of himself, his wife, Leah, knew to be a function of his illness. He seemed to her to live at a curiously obtuse angle to the realities of life. For nobody knew Robert Palmer at all. Oblique musical references, cast before an audience easily baffled by displays of verbosity, hinted at the illustrious presence of a failed musician or even composer. Talk of property and the family house in Ranelagh suggested the nobility of a fortune squandered. There was a Robert too, who was well in with diplomats and scholars and who was thought to be working on some vague long-term project. At the end of the day, he was often to be found in a corner of a pub at the top of Grafton Street in the company of the better class of homosexual. Although Leah Palmer felt that she might somehow survive her husband leaving his seed in some other woman's belly, the idea of any unorthodox wayward-ness unsettled her. The thought of him being maimed while crossing a road however, caused her anguish with-out name. She herself had the customary stock of memories appropriate to a student of the 1960s. Hours squandered in Bewley's and earnest enquiries in Gaj's Restaurant. The sense that the State might have both a future and a purpose after all. Talk of the annulment which must take place between Church and State. She had enjoyed the study of French and German and, at times, felt lacking for having given up her studies to suit the fickle-ness of her own fertility. She cherished a recollection of helping Robert in his studies with the lyrics of *lieder*. Robert fingering the subtle melodies of Wolf while she read the lyric in accompaniment. Earlsfort Terrace and discus-sions into the early hours. Before the days when the university, in dread of her sister college, shifted for safer grounds to the south of the city, where it now sat in all its emasculating anonymity among the nameless estates. She recalled a night a few months previously, when Robert had called the student up from the basement to join him in a nightcap. She had weathered their company long enough to hear her husband draw on one of those past endeavours which he conjured up from time to time to serve as a threat of future promise. The garbled narrative of the Italian scholarship he had never taken up and Leah's unfinished degree. The eyes staring out of the head as he inveigled the student into giving him ear. That frantic mannerism — his right hand tearing at the air — calling the young man closer when words alone failed to serve his intent.

—It's a while ago now, Dermot. I set a whole sequence of his poems to music. The music was devised as a sort of parallel to Thomas's words. It had to run with the magic of the words. Do you see what I'm getting at? Or, rather, do you feel what I'm getting at? This is the real question!

Over the years, Leah had learned to enmesh herself in activities so as not to give up her whole day to wondering whether her husband would surface after the day's auctioneering down at the markets. She ran a playgroup for a while and attended classes on and off. She had even toyed with the Theosophists, finally tiring of her involvement when she found herself coming to question that which she would not. When she came to work with the Samaritans, she was surprised to find that the strains in the lives of her clients provided a comforting constant against the unease of her own home. There were voices on the line each Monday and Wednesday drawing on her for counsel and an ear. The voluntary work helped her ignore the cunning which Robert had developed in order to hide his illness from himself. She no longer sought to baffle herself with responses to his oblique comments and distracted actions. By the time their second child was born, she had succeeded in acquiring a manifest indifference to both her husband's words and actions. She was never more than fleetingly aware of the silent domination which this attitude afforded her. The summer when she was heavy with Darragh, they had kept the Northern children on the spur of some casual arrangement which Robert had made. She disliked their Ulster accents and direct manner. She recalled how a pair of them had cornered Edward down by the tree-house and forced him to recite the 'Hail Mary'. The child clung to her side for the rest of their stay. Robert in his merry cups, vamping on the piano while the children sat about him on the floor singing their sour-faced songs.

—Tiger's bay was crowded, the Prods began to roar
Fifty thousand Orangemen sang 'The Sash My Father Wore',
But very soon their tune was changed to Kevin Barry's song,
When the New Lodge Road came over and it didn't take them long.

As the years turned, the one after the other, Leah came to cherish her husband's dependency. She came to view their disturbed relationship as the fruit of some secret, unspoken contract. She realised without admitting it consciously, that if her husband ever struck reason again and decided to take offence at his own drinking habits, that she might find it impossible to accommodate the man who would emerge from the fray. Robert's despondency had by now become a constant in her life. Her own suffering had come to serve her with a sense of satisfaction before the gaze of both her friends and relations. She had learned an ease of manner which, owing nothing to her husband's companionship, owed everything to his essential weakness. She was quite unprepared however, for the upset which came upon her over the Christmas break one year.

When Leah first heard that her father was whiling away the hours with another woman, she smiled at the knowledge and wondered why her mother had bothered telling her at all. Jack Wilson, her father, was an insurance broker who persisted in wearing double-breasted suits against the tides of fashion. He was a tall, insincere man who could turn the tone of his conversation to cater for all occasions. He was diaphanous of character and could duck and weave with all comers for the sake of gain. He had succeeded in disciplining himself to the extent that he could suffer ridicule and rebuff with indifference when material advantage was at stake. He cared neither for the opinions of the world nor for those of his own wife. When making a humorous remark, he signalled the moment when others should laugh with a loud coda.
—Boom! Boom!
An observer might have noticed in both his words and the blandness of his facial mannerisms, the influence of the culture of transatlantic television. His vanity denied him any sense of his own ridiculousness and so he progressed through life never lacking in confidence from one moment to the next. In the house up in Drumcondra where Leah had been reared, there had never been any pretence of devotion by either parent. She felt as though she had been fostered out to two unrelated individuals. When her father's business had been concluded down in the city, he would pass a couple of hours in the house before disappear-

ing back into the crowd again. In the early days of her courtship with her future husband, Leah discovered that Robert could identify his own chidhood in her accounts of her father's absences. They used to play verbal games with one another in cafés, inventing childhoods which had never been. The more outrageous the childhood, the more the other listened.

—And father would read Grimm to us and mother would wash the clothes in a tub by candlelight. We were poor, but we were honest.

—And we were honest, but we were poor.

At a late stage in their lives, when the word went out that the Corporation intended building nearby, Leah's parents acquired a large house on the North Circular Road at a deflated price. Each week now, Leah crossed the river to visit the solitary woman in the great house opposite the old cattle-mart. They would sit and discuss the matters of the moment while Kate played in the background. Hattie Wilson's unease with her own house was obvious. It was as though she considered herself to be merely protecting an investment by residing in the house and was not at all convinced that she should warm to the address. Leah had been standing in the garden when her mother told her the story. They were watching the child play in the thaw which had set in after the weekend blizzard. Leah had noticed that her mother appeared distressed. There had been no special treat waiting for Kate in the drawing-room. When her mother spoke, she laughed at first as though to make light of the matter.

—Your father wants to leave me, you know.

—How do you mean?

—He has found this woman, you see. I hear that she's some sort of laboratory technician.

—Who told you all this?

—Oh, yes. And she's quite a young woman. Much younger than I am.

Over the following months, Leah was obliged to pass more and more of her easy hours in the company of her mother. She stopped bringing the child with her lest the charged air of the house unsettle her. Although she had herself learned from childhood to adopt a certain aloofness when emotions raged, the visits became a strain. It was difficult to watch the eyes, stupid with relief, and the voice, alone and bewildered, without coming to question her own diligence and fidelity. There was nothing to be gained in discussing the matter with Robert. The whole business had been mentioned once or twice but there was no consolation to be found in her husband's response. In the unsettling hours of the night, when her man was heedless in sleep, Leah wondered at the cost of her own acquiescence. With one thought counselling the next and her mother's wearied smile before her in the dark, she would draw herself close enough to a conclusion to court sleep once again. She was resentful of the fact that her own upset was being felt by the children. Both boys had questioned her a number of times and she had cried quietly in front of Kate one morning. Nor was there any solace to be found in the bland formulae of redemption which Robert's mother might offer.

She found herself one evening, just before Easter, sitting in the drawing-room when Robert arrived in. The afternoon had been spent in goading her mother into seeing a solicitor the following week. By his silence she knew that her husband had spent the afternoon around town. Life lived in the mouths of small men. She followed him down to the kitchen to set the table for the evening meal. They sat facing one another as they ate, in mutual discomfort. She considered the enigma of her husband. In her mind, she sought once more to set the profanity of his illness against the gentleness he could show. There seemed to be no understanding the matter. As she set a dish of potatoes on the table before her husband, she brought to mind their first meeting. It had taken place among a gathering of mutual friends in the grounds of Trinity. Botany Bay? The Buttery? He had insisted that she go and see some Italian film with him. Bertolucci? She wasn't sure. He still retained the habit of Italian films and was upset for a week at the death by violence of Pasolini on the streets of Rome. But nowadays, music seemed to be the only medium to which his heart still had access. His outburst when she admitted to admiring the music of O'Riada during their courtship. They were in a quiet corner of the Bailey.

—Sure and it's a grand bit of music he does be writing.

—You're a snob.

—Our own Sibelius. That's what you want. Isn't it?

—What's wrong with that?

—The virtues of the peasantry. You know, in Wagner's *Lohengrin*, there's an idea called a *Frageverbot*. Hmmm? And Elsa is forbidden to ask Lohengrin, the knight of the grail, where he comes from. Or even his name. Isn't that a good idea?

Leah turned her head from the drunken man at the far side of the table. She had long puzzled over the way, unlike most others, Robert would fall to gradual silence the more he consumed. As though his mind became more and more ensnared in its own devices until it could no longer bear to whisper even the mildest discord. She recalled a night on Lake Geneva, when Edward was only a baby. A blessed flight into order for a week from the haphazardness of Dublin. It was a night which served to remind her constantly of the inarticulateness of her husband's heart. They were on a pleasure boat out on the lake at evening. An accordion in the background playing a kitsch tune for the travellers. A Bavarian couple singing along with unrepentant good humour. The simple words which touched upon her man's heart in drink.

— Schnee, Schnee, Schnee, Schnee
Tanz die ganze Nacht
Du mit Mir
Und Ich mit Dir.

The brooding introversion of his behaviour for the rest of the evening stunned her. She recalled most of all, Robert's inability to explain the nature of his distress. It was as though he were in mourning for a time gone for ever or for a land which could never be. A country of the heart whose doors had been slammed in his face.

Looking at her husband across the kitchen table again,

she realised that she must not ask the indulgence of his attention. The voices calling the Samaritans' office would distract her from her own worries for the evening. Taking her jacket from the hallstand, she called a farewell to the man below in the kitchen. There was no response. In an instant, she felt her mother's hurt embrace her with all its muted sorrow. It was an added grief to know that she might never unmask her feelings to the man whose children she had borne. It was about this time and under this particular distress, that Leah first encountered, with relief, a man other than her husband.

They met at a party, given by someone who worked for the European Commission, in a house on the Rathmines side of Ranelagh. Houses where children walked and ate slowly, untroubled by the proximity of the city. It had been late spring, although the weather was still in winter. Leah and Robert arrived to find that the party had settled into itself. The guests moved between the dining-room and the drawing-room with its great fire. Robert struck up with someone from the revenue almost as soon as they were in the door. Leah was left to herself for the moment. She watched the crowd from a distance. Civil servants and diplomats wandering about as they courted one another. There was a huddle of wives in one corner of the bare-board drawing-room. She would keep away from their number, however much they encouraged her. Later, when she thought on that moment, she could sum three notions: Robert sitting at the piano playing old Tom Lehrer songs; a paper plate laden with fresh salad which she held in her hand; the sudden awareness of a strong presence at her right shoulder. Robert playing after the style of Jelly Roll Morton which he had cultivated in his student days when playing sessions in pubs down by the gasometer. The cloying texture of the treble hand, the dancing tones of the bass. The man beside her spoke.

—That poor fellow will fall into the piano if they give him any more.

—I'll make sure they don't. Are you with Foreign Affairs?

—Not at all. Gate-crasher. Army.

—Oh.

—Worrell. Pat Worrell.

He explained that he was serving as a barrister with the army and that he had recently returned from a second tour of Lebanon.

—We stand back and let the Jews and the Arabs at it.

—What's the point in having you there at all, then?

—We supervise the collection of the dry bones, so to speak. Few of our own bones too, from time to time.

—It must be very like the North. All those factions.

—Ah, no. You have it all wrong there. The North isn't in the same league at all. It's just a barnyard scrap up there. None of this business of taking out a Prod here, a Fenian there over in the Leb. Those boys operate in tens and hundreds. Whole families and villages.

Patrick Worrell had a habit of tweaking his nose to no purpose and leaned into other people's faces when listening to them. His talk was shot through with sour wit and throwaway cynicism. He told little of himself or of his family circumstances. The loose slacks and heavy jumper he wore conspired together to hint at a physical life. His bleached hair and the annoying habit he had acquired of showing disdain by making a 'tsk' sound with tongue and teeth, must be a function of his travels, Leah felt. The cockiness and impatience with any equivocation annoyed her. Behind the carefree tones however, she detected the tongue of a rural entrepreneur shielding the reflections of a wily advocate.

—Then the Christians came along with their chains and tractor and smashed the monument to the lads. Badness. For badness. You couldn't do an act like that the honour of calling it political. And we have photographs of some of the local boys who were involved in the Sabra and Chatilla business too. Actually involved in the killings. All on file. The poor philistines get it in the neck again.

—It's very tragic.

—Still, as Jesus Christ said somewhere, 'The knackers you'll always have with you.' Isn't it a fact?

—I'm glad you think it's so funny.

—Oh, but I don't. But I have to sleep at night too. Like yourself.

She moved away from him slowly and decided to join the wives' corner to pass herself. Afterwards, when Leah watched him speak with others, she noticed the gentle limp in his right leg. And the eyes which strove to witness all and the way he listened. By the time she left the house in the early hours of the morning, Robert had fallen to his usual silence. As they lay together that night, she realised that she could not recall the christian name of the man she had met earlier on. The fact that she retained only his surname was the strongest defence she could muster against the notion which so disturbed her.

Their second meeting some weeks later, was an affair of both chance and place. Once a week, Leah would take her daughter swimming at a school for handicapped children near the city. She had often studied the hapless faces of the children and wondered at their perception of the world. Did time mean anything to them? Could they understand the meaning of good and bad? The oriental features of their faces. There was a child from the school whom they kept for weekends from time to time. A small boy from the inner city, the final burden on purse and belly in an undernourished sequence of ten. Robert's mother railed at the idea of the child visiting at all.

—Why do they have so many? Answer me that. And we're supposed to fork out for them, of course.

Leah stood chatting with Christine, the swimming instructress, as Kate played in the paddling pool. She scarcely noticed the figure doing lengths in the main pool. She stood to one side as Patrick Worrell drew himself out of the water. He chatted with the swimming instructress about the injury to his leg which he had received at a checkpoint in southern Lebanon. The woman insisted that hydrotherapy was the best treatment for the complaint. There was no doubt in her mind about that. Leah noted the abdominal scar the man bore. Appendicitis? She started slightly when the swimming instructress laid her arm on his bare shoulder. As he towelled himself, he cast about towards the child in the paddling pool, then back again to Leah.

—She's your little one, is she?

—Yes. She loves the water.

—She does alright. Still, you'd want to keep an eye on her, shallow and all as it is. Leah, wasn't it?

—Yes, that's right.

—But you're not Jewish, though?

—I'm not anything, I suppose.

—You're the same as the rest of us. Isn't that right, Christine? All heathens with no hope of salvation.

The swimming instructress smiled back at him. They watched him retire to the dressing-rooms. Christine was eager to tell more. With Kate at her side demanding to be dressed, Leah listened. She heard that Worrell's father was a publican who owned a number of lounges out in the suburbs. He himself was separated from his wife whom he kept content in an apartment down in Donnybrook. Worrell now shared the family house on Morehampton Road with his father. There were all kinds of rumours about his being involved in this and that. There was even a suggestion that there had been trouble at one stage over a smuggling venture.

—He has stories to beat the band. I wouldn't believe a word of it, though. The wife probably got tired of smelling a different perfume off him every week, I suppose. Hard thing to keep a tomcat in, they say.

The phone-call came the following week. She had just returned from leaving Kate into the crêche. She marvelled at the gall of the man in 'phoning her at home. Later on, when they came to know one another better, Worrell would hint that he had made a subtle probe into the nature of things in the house in Ranelagh before proceeding. With only the sound of the student roaming about the flat below to caution her, she agreed with a single word, to meet the following Friday morning. The intervening days were tormented by apprehension and indecision. She felt that Robert's mother might notice something and tried to avoid being left alone with her. They were to meet in a small café off Camden Street. When she arrived, Worrell was already waiting. She imagined, somehow, that the girl who took their order must mark the signs of deceit in her very manner. She listened to the man across the table from her. There was mention neither of woman nor of children. She, in her turn, talked not of home and of family, but of those activities in which she had engaged over the years. They laughed together when she mentioned the Theosophists.

—RC's, a friend of mine used to call them. Renegade Catholics, with their long faces and their mysteries.

She told of her work with the Samaritans. Worrell seemed intrigued by the idea of a voice on one end of the line giving solace to a strange voice at the other end. She declared to him that she felt a fraud sometimes, as she listened to the measures of despair and loneliness poured out to her. The youngest voices she found hardest to bear. Then too, those rural women, left alone and aloof, in one of the vast housing estates which ringed the city. These, she told Worrell, she sorrowed most for. Women from strong rural communities, left stranded with a clutch of children in schemes where there was no life between office hours. Worrell, in his turn, told her more of Lebanon. He told her of logging murderous incidents quite routinely. Of visits to the local mukhtar's house and the hills of southern Lebanon. He mentioned the summer war in the Chouf and Mount Lebanon snow-capped in the distance. He spoke of Mercedes cars gliding by peasants on donkeys and the incessant caterwauling of Arabic songs on the radio and hours spent in dusty cafés. He told of men living together and of their social order. Then he laughed at the novelty of being a legal man in a land where no writ ran.

—I used to give each group a pep-talk when they arrived at Tibnin, you see. Same thing everytime. I'd keep my eyes fixed on the most likely looking deviant in the group. Some hard chaw or other. And I'd say very solemnly to them, 'It's like this now lads — you'll be bringing them home in a suitcase with you if you as much as look at one of the local girls. And don't come running to me looking for your mammies afterwards.

When they parted, they arranged to meet again a couple of weeks later. In the house that evening, Leah found herself drifting in mood from the family about her. Robert arrived in late and she found herself oddly indifferent to his behaviour. Before he turned for sleep later on that night, he even managed to throw a gibe at her.

—Flags out tonight, Leah. Are they?

There followed a bewildered night of half-sleep and sounds heard too clearly in the stillness of her husband's sleep. Kate coughing in the next room and one of the boys making his way to the toilet. And the sound of revellers coming home from a party in the early light of the day.

Over the following weeks, they saw one another on a number of occasions. Leah was careful never to appear too elevated of spirit after these meetings. On one day they chose to meet at a busy restaurant in a shopping centre. On another afternoon, they met in a small pub on the Northside. She smiled at the twin vanities of strong coffee and tea with mint which Worrell allowed himself. She had a sense of life rousing itself from slumber in his company. She took time to see to the affairs of the house as she had always done. She insisted that Edward spend more time in the evening with his books in preparation for Glenstal after the summer. Most afternoons, she took to bringing Kate out for a stroll. She had not, as yet, confided in Worrell the detail of her parents' difficulties. She continued visiting her mother in the lonely house near the Phoenix Park and listened dutifully to what she might be told of fresh matters. Towards the end of May, Robert came down with a chest infection and she spent a long week tending him in the company of his mother. She watched her husband during those days as though from a new distance. In the man talking to himself alone at the bar, she saw the child alone in a garden keeping company with his own shadow. There was a fancy her husband had entertained as a child. He had told her about it on numerous occasions. It had sounded a resonance in the memories of her own childhood. The idea that he was the only one alive in the world. A small child, in an empty garden. His mother watching from the window.

The way the years and his weakness had left their tale on his features was suddenly quite apparent. How the suits and ties scarcely served to conceal any longer the distress the mind and body suffered. The subtle practice of self-deceit was mirrored in the attention the man paid to his dress each morning. The ritual of choosing a tie each day. His dark hair cross-combed into silken submission. Leah kept her hours with the Samaritans as before, for the comfort of routine was a settling certainty on days when doubt and anxiety crowded her thoughts.

On one grey morning of a damp mid-week in June she met Worrell in a pub on a mountain road up past Rathfarnham. They had taken to exchanging small tokens of affection now. As she drove out from the social fastness of Ranelagh, through its well-mannered sister suburbs, Leah fingered the prayer beads Worrell had given her on their last meeting. A chain of olive beads strung together with hemp. Robert's mother had left earlier that week for her annual break with some in-laws of her late husband in west Cork. She would stay in the small hotel which they owned. She took Katie with her for company and both Leah and Robert would drive down to collect them the following weekend. Leah dreaded the trip. There would be the drive along the pitted roads of west Cork. Then the inevitable confusion over signposts. In the hotel, Robert's mother would be seated, gaunt and demanding in a circle of her own, rambling on about her son and life in the city. Leah would stay in the background, keeping an eye on the children. Robert could pass the day with his uncle. The arguments would start when it was time to leave and the inevitable decision to spend the night in the hotel would follow.

Leah left the car in the car park to the rear of the pub, where it would be least conspicuous. Worrell stood up to greet her when she entered the lounge. An onlooker would have surmised that the children of such a union would be strong and dark and not given to sedentary ways. She noted once again, the air of certainty in the man's talk. How he never appeared too anxious to refer to the past nor appeared to believe that the future warranted anything but the scantest attention. He kissed her lightly on the cheek as they rose to leave. They left her car by the pub and drove off in the direction of Glencree. Afterwards, Leah could recall every cold detail of the morning. The light rain which fell along the way as they passed the old reformatory and the German cemetery. The scattered couples walking the mountain road towards the youth hostel. A man and a boy out cutting turf on the bog. The lark she heard when she stepped out of the car in front of the chalets. Worrell explained to her that a German friend, who had had a barring order taken out against him by his wife, allowed him use the chalet to come and go as he pleased. Passing a group of children playing about on a grass patch, Leah turned away from them on instinct. Inside, Worrell lit a gas heater. There was a smell of damp wood and wet summer. There was no sound now but the odd car on the road outside and the children running about. Each cold detail she could later recall. As Worrell had told her he could recall each word, each face, each object associated in his mind with the night the Israelis invaded Lebanan.

—This is the thing, Leah. All the side issues fall away. In the face of death. You're left with the idea that you are alive. Intensely alive. The sensation is staggering. Adrenalin, you see. Blood sugar levels too. Chemical conscious. And what detail sticks out in my mind above all else that night? A packet of halwa — of this sweet sesame seed stuff — lying on a case of ammunition. And the earth shaking above our heads.

Her skin was alive to his touch. They lay down on the bed behind the partition. His hands, rough to the world. Her tears almost starting then when her womb shuddered. Sleep after relief and relief after release. The sounds on the air outside. The light through the window above their heads. She heard a child's voice calling another 'coward'.

A lark dancing on the air above their heads somewhere. The damp fervour of the moment. She reached for the angora sweater and drew it over her breasts. The inevitability of it all. His arms were around her as she sat, rocking backwards and forwards, hands over her ears as though to drown out his words. His full and frantic seed running from her as she stood to dress. Worrell was calling to her from the kitchen area. There was a smell of coffee and the taint of dulling gas on the air. The song he lilted in mockery. His laughter as he watched the children through the glass.

— Oh take it down from the mast
Irish traitors
It's the flag we Republicans claim
It will never belong to Free-Staters
For they brought on it nothing but shame.

Over the summer, they met regularly. She had plenty of time to consider the days on which she had been visited by the desire to leave her husband. It was odd, she thought, that the reaction had always been stronger when they were out of Dublin. There was a night in Paris, when they had taken advantage of a cheap ticket from one of Robert's contacts. They would have the week to themselves with no children to worry about. They had started off around Sacre Coeur one afternoon intending to return to the pension by tea. By late evening it was clear that Robert must carry on drinking until unconsciousness or sickness halted his progress. The stench of brandy and anis on his breath angered her. They lost themselves in a maze of side streets and ended up in the immigrant quarter of Barbes. The eyes of the north African Arabs on their drunken progress. There she had sworn, as they stood quarrelling in the Metro with the smell of urine at their throats, that she would take steps on her return to Dublin. She found it hard to face the puzzle of her indecision the following morning. She might allow herself believe that she had become dependent on her husband's misfortune, but she could not easily credit the fact that she had come to learn the art of domination by the subtle manipulation of the terms of her husband's illness. She was generally unaware of that deviousness which she had adopted as a strategy for survival in the face of alcoholism. She did understand however, that she was now beginning to develop two contrasting and complementary sides to her character now. With the younger children in the summer scheme, Leah had the earlier part of the day to herself. There were whole mornings she passed with Worrell in the chalet up in the mountains. Sometimes too, they would meet in small cafés on the fringes of the city. There, they would coax one another along, laughing about the ways of the world and the stories of the day. Leah liked to simulate shock at the coarseness of her companion's talk.

—These ones came into the bar, you see.

—Women?

—Well, dear Jesus, but they were all but lying up on the table and the big mammy dugs on them.

—Breasts, Pat. They're called breasts. Dug is for a beast.

—Well, it was cat melodeon, boy. Every whore in the place must have heard that the Paddies were in town with the few bob to spend.

—And what did you do?

—Shag all we could do, Leah. Says I to my CO, let them fly in their own penicillin when they get back to Ballyfermot after the tour. Am I my brother's brothel keeper? Was it for this the wild geese spread the grey wing? Forget it. We just got offside and let them get on with it.

Sometimes she wrong-footed herself in the company of her husband, surprising him with her fresh enthusiasm for things. There were other days on which she told herself that she must terminate the whole business for once and for all. On such days, she inevitably found herself alone in the drawing-room at evening, driven by simple remorse into praying that she would be found out soon and that she would be punished in some way for her deviousness.

In July, she spent a week with the family in a small hotel near Westport. Robert's mother came with them on account of her son's recent illness. The woman made much of giving her son and his wife a chance to spend a few hours together. In reality, they passed little time in one another's company. Robert settled into a daily scheme of things and Leah was free to wander off in the afternoons as she would. She watched one night in the hotel bar as her mother-in-law had Robert take the podium and play for her before the crowd. The hand brushing the hair back off the forehead, the steady composure of his smile when speaking into the microphone.

—And for my mother there by the door, a gentle mutation of a piece by Chopin which she claims to love. First the white notes.

After the laughter and the tune, a little trick to show his versatility at the keyboard. He played a common tune, whose melody was couched in a sharp key and whose bass accompaniment was told in a flat key. Leah heard the delighted applause of the crowd. She saw Robert's mother at the table nearest the piano, garnering the compliments on her son's talent. Sitting back in her chair as though receiving tribute. The infinite sweetness of watching failure applaud itself. When the joke dragged on, the audience grew disenchanted and Robert left the keyboard with ill-humour. On more than one occasion during the week by the sea, Leah teased herself with the prospect of quitting both men at once. Then, she would be faced with the curious feeling that the matter would resolve itself in the run of the year and that she might do nothing now to halt its progress. Back in the city after the break, she found that her father had left the house on the North Circular Road for good and that he had taken up residence with his companion in an apartment in Ballsbridge. Her mother seemed to be reconciling herself to the new situation quite well. By now, a new coldness had entered into the older woman's heart and some of her former dignity had returned. On the strength of Leah's advice, her mother began to prepare herself mentally for the courts and the unseemly. Leah smiled at the change in her mother. Poor Hattie Wilson, who loved to cry about life, seemed to be finding a new sense of purpose with her husband's rejection. She had even said to Leah — was she joking? — that if separated through the courts, she would join a widows' club and throw it in Jack Wilson's face. Life without her husband now seemed an altogether invigorating proposal. Hattie Wilson still chewed her butterscotch drops noisily, but no longer walked about her own house as though she were waiting on someone. She took an interest in the garden again and gave into vanity by refusing to wear spectacles in company. She resembled less and less a misplaced piece of chipped bone china. She took her fussy chihuahua for a walk each day in the Phoenix Park and sometimes declined to meet her daughter for lunch on the grounds of a previous engagement. It was clear to Leah that her mother was no longer prey to the enthusiasms of vegetarians, Rosicrucians and consciousness-raising schemes. No longer did her home resemble, as it had always done, a house which had been rearranged by the relatives of a recently bereaved person for the purposes of a quick sale. When her husband 'phoned her in a skittish humour about some papers he wanted forwarded though the post, she was firm with him. The jittery timbre of her voice was at odds with the strength of her words.

—And you can hump off, Jack. You can damn well come and get them yourself, if you like. You know the address. Or maybe what's-her-name would oblige you?

As the 'phone was replaced in its cradle in the house on the North Circular Road, Jack Wilson looked about him in astonishment at the woman reading the magazine on the couch. When Hattie Wilson did not return his call within the hour with an apology, it finally occurred to him that his wife might be rejecting him. Even in the depths of drunkeness later on that evening, he declined to divulge to his new companion the details of the mortal slight which he had suffered at the words of his wife.

Sometime after Edward started his first term at Glenstal, Leah had her first row with Worrell. They met that morning in a café to the south of the city. Worrell had just returned from a conference in Galway. He brought a present for her of a fine, silver chainlet.

—You've a real little wren's bone of a wrist, so you have.

Afterwards, they drove up the mountains. It was the first morning she had met the owner of the chalet. Worrell told her on the way of a raid on one of his father's pubs which stood near a Corporation estate.

—Sure, God love them, aren't they only stealing back what he robs off of them every day of the week.

They were scarcely in the door of the chalet when they heard the sound of a car with a faulty exhaust wheezing its way into the car park. Then the little German was standing before them. Leah was immediately put off by the man's matter-of-fact acceptance of her presence. She fell to silence. When he had left, Worrell told her of the incident which had led to the German's being barred from his house. One evening, when he should have been working, he took a taxi up to some disco outside Tallaght on a tip-off. There, he caught his wife out and brought her outside to the car park to give her a beating before the eyes of the taxi-man. Worrell turned about from the sink to cap his tale, his eyes starting out of his head as he imitated the taxi-man's tones.

—Ah, I couldn't take money from a man who was only doing his duty. I won't let on I seen anything.

Leah left the cup to one side. She watched the rain hurl itself against the window behind Worrell.

—Why are you telling me this, Pat?

—It's a story, Leah. Franz's little story. Not Leah's.

—It's not funny.

—I didn't say it was.

—Then why are you laughing?

The row drew breath from there. In a moment, there were screams followed by tears and a silent drive down the mountain again. They didn't meet for several weeks, until it was almost Hallowe'en. The intense loneliness which she felt in the company of her own family now distressed Leah greatly. She had little patience with Kate. Robert, who had been generally unwell during the course of the summer, was diagnosed as having some sort of mineral deficiency. She felt the old raging at her man's illness take hold of her once again. The voices on the line no longer served to comfort her. Voices telling their own tales of despair. A young girl's voice — a suicide's voice — calling out to her from the depths of misery. When she watched Robert move about the house now, she wondered why she had never thought to cry her own cold grief before.

When she began seeing Worrell again, they were more cautious with one another initially. Then, almost without noting it, the caution gave way to bemused indifference. They even met on one occasion in a pub in the centre of town frequented by the younger town house people who might have recognised her. She met with Worrell's father on the steps of the house in Morehampton Road one day. The small, breathless man in the homburg scarcely admitted to seeing her and directed his comments to his son instead.

—You'll catch your death in that jacket. Wouldn't you go and buy yourself a decent coat, for Christ's sake? You're back in Paddyland now, you know. Not over tanning your arse in the promised land.

On a dark rainy day, she turned a corner onto Grafton Street and almost collided with her father and his companion. The woman was tall and, like herself, dressed in a loose skirt and top. Her father's eyes were beaming.

—Patricia, Leah.

—Hello.

—We're meeting up with Charlie Boland for a quick one in Neary's. Better rush on. How's the bold Robert?

—He's fine.

—.Good. Good. See you about then. Love to all.

The woman looked back over her shoulder at Leah as they departed and smiled. For a moment, Leah was dumbstruck by the sense of unreality the encounter had evoked in her. The woman's tidy features lingered as an afterimage in her mind. Her father's manner amused her. His face smitten with schoolboy devil-may-care, his skin puffed up with vanity. Love had added by stealth to the azure arrogance of his eyes the sweetened smile of a fool.

At Christmas, Edward arrived home from boarding school. Although Leah had noticed no great change in the boy during the Hallowe'en break, now she did. He had learned, in much the same way as she herself had done over the years, to ignore Robert. To avoid hurt. The holiday passed quietly and, in the first days of the new year, they left Edward back to school. She recalled passing through Limerick. The decay evident in the face of the city and the deadness of its inhabitants. Her thoughts, on the return journey, were of her eldest son alone. She scarcely spoke to Robert until they reached Dublin. She was content in the knowledge that she had resisted the impulse to confide her emotions in the boy. That desire, which had almost won her reason more than once, to sit down with him and tell of life and the living which must be done with it. She upbraided herself with the realisation that a certain shame had stayed her tongue. She marvelled at the pulse of manhood evident in the boy's every move. The subtle arrogance of his smile intrigued her. She missed her first child and neither the clumsy warmth of her second son nor the follies of her small daughter could take his place.

As the new year drew on, Leah found herself sulking more and more in the company of those around her. On the heels of a minor scene with a colleague, she withdrew temporarily from the Samaritans. Now she imagined that she spent whole days avoiding her mother-in-law about the house. When the old woman took ill with bronchitis, it was all Leah could do to serve the woman her meals in bed. She suspected now and then, that the old woman knew by her awkwardness and unease that some alien name lurked behind the scenes. She surprised herself with the realisation that she longed for the old stability of things in some unreckoned way. For the younger children at their hour in the garden and Edward upstairs at his books. For Robert's mother fussing over the sweet cherry and the privet. For Robert himself, sauntering in to deliver some garbled message culled from a meeting with his own. For voices on the line, bearing their saddening embassies to her and the odd relief this brought. When she was finally taken to task by the quiet keeper of the house, she knew that one escapade above all others that spring had set her husband's sentinel on the watch. And she understood too, that she might have conspired against herself unconsciously, in order to bring about her own downfall and a timely resolution to the affair.

Just before Easter, Leah announced to the house that she had decided to enrol in a weekend residential course to be held in the west. A girlfriend, from the days of Earlsfort Terrace, would accompany her. The course related to self-development and would be hosted by an American lecturer. Robert appeared altogether indifferent to the idea although his mother expressed amusement at the plan. She gave it out at the breakfast table, that she believed such courses were peddled as a surrogate for organised religion. She confessed to some surprise at her daughter-in-law's sudden show of gullibility. Arrangements were finalised. On a bright Friday morning, the two women left the city. At Hayden's in Ballinasloe Leah took her travelling companion into her confidence and was momentarily thrown by her intemperate response. They spoke little to one another for the rest of the journey to Clifden. The town of Clifden, created *ex nihilo* for the diversion of the gentry in the previous century, had been granted a new importance by the presence of French tourists on its streets during the summer. It had little reference to its surroundings. For those who visited it during the high season, there was a comforting sense of being elsewhere. Leah cast an eye over the participants. They would be for the most part women from the southern suburbs of Dublin and the city of Galway. Women who would feel comfortable with the aura of north Connemara, away from the anarchy of the uncouth south. She waited in the lounge of the hotel. When Worrell finally arrived they left directly. They would spend the weekend in a small house which lay a few miles outside the town.

—I wonder when this place last saw a decent fire?

A small rowing-boat lay in the middle of the floor, keel upwards. They carried it outside and lit a fire against the chill of the evening. With the last light of the day, they took a walk down by the strand. Passing a small stream on the way, Worrell pointed out a salmon net slung across a culvert. A heron, solemn and watchful, took to the air before their eyes. While Leah gathered shells, Worrell contented himself with strolling along and listening. It seemed to him that the silence was too oppressive for her. Her words threatened the stillness of the evening. She stopped to settle the combs in her hair. They faced one another.

—I wish someone would tell me what to do, Pat.

—Like you used to? On the 'phone.

—In a way.

—And what would you like to be told?

—I have no idea.

They ate a meal of mackerel, potatoes and tinned vegetables. When they had tired of talking, they lay down. Leah woke first, to the unnerving silence and the presence of the man beside her. Running her hand along his back, she thought over something she had heard on the radio one evening. Of the banishment of quiet and the invention of sounds which had never been heard before. That was an interesting idea. She sat up in bed and watched the sleeping man beside her. His shallow breathing was scarcely audible. How life seemed to function as a goal for him and how it served only to depress others. There were only two modes to Patrick Worrell's life, she decided. There was either the intensity of wakefulness or the deep relief of sleep. What was he doing with her at all? As a ploy to tease out her own thoughts, she stripped the man beside her of a name. Who was he then? She lay her hand upon the bleached hair on the nape of his neck. He was a free spirit whom she had met by chance. They would part by chance. There was nothing banal about that, she felt. They might even enjoy one another's company for another while yet. But she would not allow herself be consumed by him. The physical facts of their liaison did not trouble her. There was nothing to be marvelled at there. A drunken reminiscence of Robert's, when he had spent a summer in Paris as an undergraduate with a girlfriend, set her smiling.

—A series of exchanges was effected. Oh, I was full of it for the next year. The idea was quite new in those days of course.

The act of allowing the strange man beside her prowl about her thoughts was more unsettling. The sense of giving him house-room in her heart. She sought vainly to shock herself: what was the betrayal in a simple act of insemination? The strange man beside her stirred. He appeared to be on the last reaches of sleep. Her fingers danced along his back. Piano fingers. Long thin fingers I have, like Robert's. Melody in my head again. What is that tune?

—How deep is the night
No moon tonight
No friendly star
To guide me with its light
Be still my heart!

That was where she last recalled him playing it. It hadn't been in Westport at all. She was alone in the bedroom at evening. She had retired early with biscuits and a book and aspirin. She tried to frame the moment. Let me see: everyone asleep except us. Robert's mother and all the children in bed. Just myself and Robert. Alone, separated by walls. He, below in the drawing-room. I, above in bed. The strange man beside her drew himself out of sleep to smile at her, but she turned away anxious lest the memory be doused without recall.

—So deep is the night
O lonely night.

Robert's fingers at the keyboard. Felt he was playing for me and he knew I was listening too. Because he could not talk to me. I said: I will dress and go downstairs and sit with him even if I cry. But I did not. I lay in bed and cried quietly instead, knowing that the melody twined about his fingers was mine as well as his.

When Worrell drew her about to face him, the memory fled and was no more. They fell together leisurely and rose at midday and left the chalet. They spent the afternoon driving along the coast to the south. In the sunlit alcove of a small pub in the islands, she came to speak of the man who was her husband and of his burden. They were ignored by the dark-suited men at the bar with their heavy, mumbling tongue. Neither the dog snoozing under the dartboard nor the man leaning on the counter reading the *Independent* gave them eye.

—But why him? Why my Robert?

—And not some blackguard who deserved it?

—I suppose that's what I'm saying.

—.Why famine? Why war? Why sick children? Is that not the same question?

—That's too mystical for me, Pat. Don't make fun of me.

She felt the gin touching her tongue. There was something, she said, which her mother used to whisper to her about an aunt who became depressed with gin. The more she cries, the less she pisses. She fell asleep in the car, waking up as they turned in off the road for the house. They ate out in a hotel near Clifden. Over dinner, Worrell told her that he had signed on for another tour of duty in the autumn. Leah was immediately stricken by a premonition of the end of things and the prospect of change once again. She scarcely followed the anecdote about the swearing in of the FCA recruits in Griffith Barracks. And she would not cry. She looked up from her plate.

—And have you told Orla yet?

—Not yet. I wanted to tell you first.

—I feel honoured.

She passed their last night uneasy in sleep and lay a long while on the bright morning, mulling over the matter of the night before. The day moved by in moody silences before Leah met up with her friend for the drive back across the midlands to Dublin. Neither woman said much on the road although, when they stopped for a meal in Ballinasloe, Leah's friend consented to giving her an account of the course along with some printed material. Robert was in the kitchen with the children when she arrived home. His mother had gone to bed early, having come down with a cold the previous day. When the children had been put to bed she retired herself. For a while, they sat up talking. Robert spoke of some minor politician he had run into around town on the Friday night. He gave his wife a letter from Glenstal which he had left unopened. Wondering, in their sleeping embrace, whether marriage might indeed be possible, Leah's thoughts were troubled only by the heavy slumber of the woman in the adjoining room.

It was a few days before the old woman finally struck. Leah could recount the setting without much effort. They were down in the breakfast room. Robert had left an hour earlier for the markets and she had just seen Darragh off to school and the student had joined her. Kate was romping about at their feet. The fine weather of the previous few days had held and she had decided to bring the child to the park after breakfast. The student was setting her a riddle. Something about a tortoise and a hare. It was one of Zeno's paradoxes, he told her. They were marching their fingers up and down the breakfast table trying to solve the riddle. The student was clapping his hands in goodnatured mockery. His head of fair hair haloed in the morning light.
—You'll never solve it like that, Mrs Palmer. Not a hope in heaven.
His eyes moved towards the presence by the door. Robert's mother was smiling discreetly at him. The child ran towards the old woman. Leah stood up to wet fresh tea while the student, uneasy now under the gaze of the intruder, hastened to finish his breakfast. He told Leah that he would give her until the following morning to sort out the puzzle and bade a restrained farewell. Leah had marked the old woman's mood from the moment she set idle foot into the bright room. The studied certainty of her movements as she sat to table. Her coldness with the child. They spoke together briefly on the forthcoming folk evening in Darragh's school. There would be singing and dancing, a short play in which Darragh had a part and some humorous sketches. Sister would conduct the choir and the canon would open the evening. Robert's mother had never approved of the children attending the school, so Leah made little of the woman's disinterest. As she

stood to tidy away the breakfast vessels, she thought back to the three-cornered row which had taken place some years before when they had first enrolled Edward at the Church of Ireland school. They had been in the drawing-room. She had been carrying Darragh at the time. The bitterness of her mother-in-law's tongue. Trying to divide them.

—You have to follow fashion, I suppose. But, I'm surprised at you, Robert.

From the breakfast window, Leah could see the postman. She called out to Kate and the child made her way up the stairs to collect the letters. It was as she turned to dry her hands on the kitchen towel that the old woman spoke. She chose not to look up from her newspaper as she did so. Her words came almost as the herald of some innocuous afterthought.

—Do you think me a fool, Leah?

The paper was lowered and their eyes were upon one another. The coldness in the glance. Leah paused a moment. She thought to leave the room before the woman could continue, but she did not move.

—Do you think I haven't got eyes and ears and a brain, Leah?

The child was stumbling down the stairs now. She was trying to count the letters as she did. Confusing letters with steps and steps with letters. Calling out to Leah to come and help her. Leah left the tea-towel aside and made towards the stairs. The voice followed her.

—Do you think I'm going to watch you treat my own flesh and blood like that and turn a blind eye? Do you hear me, girl!

She comforted the fallen child and, gathering up the letters, ascended the stairs clutching the small hand tightly. Her mother-in-law's excited words trailed her into the drawing-room. Of her son and her grandchildren and the black deceit of the heart. Of the fruits of poor rearing and the word she would put in Robert's ear that very evening.

They were together in the drawing-room now. Leah looked into the mirror over the mantelpiece at her husband. His hands were fidgetting with the embroidery of the armrest. She knew it for a nervous habit which struck whenever silence told on him. They watched one another through the impartial medium of the mirror, their images dulled now by the shadows in the sky. Leah looked down into the garden below the window. At the spindly limbs of the cherry tree; at the garish Forsythia and its brazen blaze of yellow, by the garden gate. She thought of the older woman who had just left the room and of the warm, safe abode she had secured for herself in the past. She hoped Kate would not wake again and the moment be lost forever. She thought of the man sitting beside her and of the questions he might ask. All the whys and wherefores necessary to round off the whole business. The tie loosened at the neck, the head buried in the hands. She had neglected to water the houseplants too. By the door, on a low mahogany stand, she could see the insidious Cyclamen. Its long limbs reaching out to all about it. A present from Robert. Something he had dragged back from the market one day on top of a crate of apples. She recalled his shyness when presenting her with the plant. There too, on the coffee-table, stood the dowdy, blighted geranium which Robert's mother was so fussy about. Lavender and sealing-wax and the *Daily Mail*. That was Mrs John Palmer alright. Her husband coughed. In the mirror, she saw him rise and cross slowly to the piano. She stubbed her cigarette out in an ashtray on the mantelpiece. They were lost to one another for a moment. Robert's fingers tipped the tarnished keys and a sour interval stabbed the air. Where was his mind now? She wondered at the turn of his thoughts.

Augmented fourth. What was it they used to call it? *Mi contra fa diabolus est in musica*. Banned by the church. Something to do with orgies. Steady, menacing rise and fall of tones. Things I want to say to you, Leah, but Jesus knows I can't. The questions I would ask you!

—His eyes?

—Blue, like yours, Robert. His skin burns easily.

I am alone, Leah. Always alone. Child in a silent room.

Child in an empty garden. They drift away from me at the bar. The children even. Are they afraid of me? Darragh is just an innocent and Kate has your smile. And Edward? You do hate me, Edward. Don't you? And will you inherit this burden from me? What a price to pay for being my son!

—How long have ...?

—A year. Perhaps a little more. We met at a party. You were there too.

It is as though I had been lowered into a pit of loneliness over the years and left there, Leah. Other day, standing on the podium in the fruit market. Little gutty from Skerries in front of me giving lip about the price of something. I said to myself: Why am I here? What am I doing here, with men of no moment? Ah, college. Life danced and sang. Funny little row I had with someone in the music department. Boydell? What was it over, now? Something to do with one of the moderns. Nielsen, I think. Now, what? All that atonal dissonance. I never liked it. Oh, the glorious smugness of youth. Now, what? My fingers stiff and my ear atrophied. Manage every now and then to follow a score where once — I swear it — I could compose inverted counterpoint as I listened to a melody.

—How did he touch you? I mean...

—We were as man and woman together.

Thing I read once about the whores in old Les Halles in Paris. Special part of their bodies which they reserved for their 'mecs'. Oh, *nolle me tangere, fils de putre*! Why can I not say that I am hurt? Why have I never been able to say that? 'Life is such and had to be lived.' I see my mother's smiling face at the door when I fall in the garden. No Veronica there. Never to cry pain. Weakness.

—And what words did you call out in love?

—Jesus! Oh, love! Jesus!

All things collapsing. The city even. Last days of my father. After the stroke. We used to sit him out in an armchair in the sun, like a child. Do you remember? Newspaper in his hands as a useless prop. Hat angled awkwardly on his head. Children peering over the walls at the scarecrow who mumbled when he wanted to be brought in.

What went on in your mind, father? And do you ask the same about me, Leah? Questions I would ask.

—Why must I know about this at all, Leah?

—Because life is pain. By pain we know that we live. But your mother has told you this already.

Her husband coughed behind her. She heard the piano lid being closed again. Their eyes scarcely crossed as she turned to give him a cigarette. She thought of the chalet in the mountains, up above the vast bewildered estates of west Dublin. She recalled gathering flowers by the roadside. Speedwell, Herb Robert and some other yellow flower. Hedge mustard? Looking down upon the spread of houses creeping up to the very foot of the mountain.

—Tallaght. The suburb that dare not speak its name.

That was funny. Pat Worrell's little joke. No. No. Children there. Robert then. Robert's little joke. She bent forward to take a light. Then the man who was not her husband was among her thoughts once more. His talk. Death crouching behind the pallisades of a concrete bunker in southern Lebanon. The awesome moment of his words when telling a story. The residue of the frantic East in his eyes as they rounded a bend on the Military Road. The comfort of the cycle of things assailing her once again. The knowledge that what had been might be again. Of the cycle of the seasons and each day claiming its fellow in quiet unanimity. As she stood, watching her husband in the mirror, she began to welcome anew the set purpose of the affairs of her life. A son arriving home from boarding school anxious to please. An old woman weathering the days with loud forebearance. Shaken voices on the line demanding comfort. Robert, a man-child, unable to rest after the hour of seven in the morning. Chattering to the children below in the breakfast room. The tidy remove she had learnt over the years in her dependence on him. Perhaps she needed his illness by this stage now. Dependence worked both ways. Wasn't that true? The thing was, that the man in the room with her did not want to know of what had happened. He could probably live content with the assumption that she might again find favour with another.

But he must not hear of it. There must be no pain. They might agree on that between themselves, without saying a word. Not toiling over the past nor tormenting themselves with days not yet realised. The certainty of all in the turning of the wheel, in the lifting of the glass. She waited for her husband to speak, but no words came.

Must leave this room, Leah. And hide. You know that. You understand that. Go into town and speak to someone. Maybe in the Horse and Tram. Cinema crowd. Should be someone there. Or up in the Shakespeare. County council lot. Slip in among them and lose myself for a few hours. There was a song you used to help me with once. Remember? Wolf? Yes, Wolf. Christ, you were so young. Sitting by the piano, chanting the words as I played. How long ago? *Lass, O Welt, O lass mich sein!* You said it was a despondent song. Were all *lieder* like that, you asked. No, I said. Only the ones I warm to. Touch of the words. If you could only hear them.

—Let me be, O world!
Do not tempt me with gifts of love
Let this heart keep to itself
Its joy and its sorrow.

He looked up from the armchair. They had neglected to appease the dullness of the evening with light and were both enshrouded with the gloom now. He heard his wife speak.

—Well?

She looked at the man. His hands were resting on his knees. His lips were pursed as an altar boy fretting for a cue not resolved. She marked the heaviness of the eyes and felt tears braiding her own cheeks. As he lay his head against her, she heard Kate move upstairs in the bed. The old woman's voice called out across the stillness. Leah thought of the virus which had been moving among the children in the crêche over the past couple of weeks. And then she worried contentedly over the way of things and the many names people will use when speaking of the one matter.

The Africa Room

SHE WAS UNABLE, after all, to go back to bed. As she stood by the whinging kettle, she took herself to task for allowing the boy out alone into the early morning. He would have left the laneway now. He should be crossing over by the tannery fields leading down to the river. The light was rising on the day. He would, at least, be able to see his way. She cursed herself once more for even suggesting the venture. As she rose the kettle to wet the tea, she heard footsteps on the staircase. She pretended not to hear the child opening the kitchen door. The small hands scouring half-sleep from the eyes. She turned around and started in mock surprise. The child ran across the floor and raised her arms to be lifted.

—That bold woman gave her mammy a fright!

—Where's Tom going?

The dogs barking in the yard told the oddness of the morning. They were at the door. The child could hear their paws upon the wood. Perhaps the child's voice had aroused them. They had not been bothered when she and the boy had been arguing a little while earlier. Even the dogs, she felt, would have grown accustomed over the years to the coarse cut of the early morning rows in the house. As they had all done. Since she had succeeded in having the man barred from the house, there had been little to argue about. Just the normal differences of families. She set the child up on the kitchen table and threw a jacket about her shoulders. There was little point in trying to go back to bed now. Nobody would be able to sleep. The other children were probably lying awake in their beds, fretting over what they had heard of the argument. It would have reminded them of older days. Of days when the man cultivated searing rows on the turn of a single word. Mornings ravaged by bad tongues and evil intentions. There had not been a broken morning like this in a long while. The child helped herself down off the table, to fetch the kindling from a cardboard box. She rapped on the door as she passed and laughed as the dogs outside responded. When the fire finally took, the dogs were let in. The collie was the friskier of the two. The labrador was content to lie before the flames and watch the child at play. The woman set the kettle on the stove once again, having emptied the pot of its lukewarm tea. Then she sat herself at the table and took up the evening newspaper she seemed to have scarcely left down. Perhaps the others had taken sense and gone back to sleep. She would explain all later on. As she turned the pages, drifting from one face to the next, she harried herself once again for having allowed the boy out at all.

The tannery fields, drenched in dew, had saturated his trousers. He paused a moment by the sheep dip to try and brush some of the lighter fall from his legs. Ahead of him, in the distance, he could see the chalet. There was no sign of anyone. The sun was lifting now and, feeling its force, he knew that it would be another strong summer's day. As the day before had been. He had gone down through the fields the previous day, to swim in the poaching hole. He had taken care though not to go anywhere near the chalet, lest he should chance on either the man or the woman. Down near the poaching hole where, his mother told him, the dippers used to come to baptise people once upon a time. It had been a long time since he had last spoken to the man. He was given sound instructions not to be taken in by his sweetness. Not even on the street. He was not to answer questions either. Now the boy spent all his spare hours helping out in the family grocery when his mother was out of the shop. He could see a couple of grazers sitting out by the line of trees to the rear of the chalet. Staring dazedly into the face of the sun, they did not hear his footsteps until he was practically upon them. Then they scattered and made for the maybushes once more. He halted a few yards from the chalet and wondered what he should do. It occurred to him that they might both have made a mistake. Perhaps they had heard nothing after all. Any sound or silence could take on a thousand different names in that dawn reach which lay between sleep and waking. They had argued over what they had heard. His mother thought that she had counted two shots, while he was certain that he had heard only one. Perhaps his sleep had been heavier than hers. He cautioned himself against thinking anymore about what might lie before him. There was his mother's counsel, which had bidden him to stay and let the business sort itself out. Then there was his own desire to bring the matter to earth as soon as possible. As he began to move towards the chalet once more, he knew that he did not care very much about how he might find his father. Nor did he have any sympathy for the woman who shared his bed. He realised that he had taken on the errand as a simple unspoken favour for his mother alone.

When she was sure that the child on the settee was falling to sleep, she took down her own jacket from the door and draped it over her. Then she hunted the dogs back into the yard. She left the connecting door to the shop ajar lest the child, waking suddenly, should find her gone and fret. She kept her own hand from the light switch. Someone passing might notice and, thinking something was amiss, call the guards. A van went by to meet the early morning train from Dublin and the 'papers. She rummaged about in the dark musty silence of the shop for the packet she had left in one of the drawers. She lit the first cigarette of the morning and, leaning against the counter, savoured the sharp cut of the saltpetre against the smells of fresh vegetables and dried teas. It was hard to counter the mood which would drive her out down by the fields after her son. She told herself that she could not leave the child alone in the kitchen while the others slept. That she must wait. If he hadn't arrived back by the time the others rose for school she would go off down by the lane herself and see. As the early light insinuated its way through the small cracks in the blinds, the woman set to tidying the shop for the day's commerce. She wondered as she worked at the way things fell in life. With the man driven from the house now, things had settled down once more. The tribute exacted of her nerves over the years was ended. There was undisturbed sleep again in the house. The madness which had afflicted Tom, her eldest, seemed to be in abeyance. How the boy's childhood had been sorrowed by his father's shadow. The man, drunk and demanding, calling her whore before her son. The troubles the boy would visit upon himself in his despair. Poor work in school. One incident after another. She recalled something about something daubed on the walls of the chapel. The sacristan in the sitting-room. Words with herself and her husband. How her husband had caught the boy in the barn later on that day. The raw wounds she had bathed that night. Then the man roaring into the house, in the early hours of the morning, to exact retribution of his wife for the embarrassment caused to his name down the town. There was the company the boy had nosed out too. Those from the council estate, who went home to mugs of tea and jam sandwiches for dinner. The day she took the boy aside to try and speak to him.

—If you lie with dogs, Tom, you'll get up with fleas.

Now things had grown calm once again. There was little mention of the man in the house. Occasionally, one of the children might catch sight of him out in the street or making his way down the laneway at night. Tales they would have heard around the town about their father. The talk when he first took the chalet and brought in some half-whore from Kilkenny, who had reneged on both her husband and children. She had caught a glimpse of the woman a few times. Stumbling along with her own man in the distance. The same shadow in her features. The frantic search for solace in oblivion. She had often thought of the life they must live. A dazed, confounded world, disinherited of all order and reason. Violent tongues, where even silence raged. She pondered on how the woman's body ran with the shadow. The very sense of her rhythms was so distracted, she reasoned, that there was probably no fear of her being burdened. As she swept behind the counter, she considered the thousand nights she had worried over the man's ways. How, even when he had left and set up house with the strange woman, she worried that death might take him suddenly. By fire on a star-lit night; by drowning on a night when the moon hid her face. She stooped to pick up a toy car by the freezer. She knew that she should not have allowed the boy to go alone to query the disturbance. The child in the kitchen had awoken and was calling her now. She left the brush to one side and went in from the shop. Cuddling the girl in her arms, she puzzled over the matter. Had she suggested to the boy that he go out, or had he decided on that strategy himself? She wasn't sure. With the child still in her arms, she drew back the curtains on the gable window. But she could see nothing and the speck that was the chalet would be hidden by the bushes near the river anyway. She should not have allowed the boy out.

A black cat ran out from the wooden house. The boy skirted the front door, which lay open, and made for the bedroom window. It would not be right to walk in on his father and the woman. His father might take fright and go for him. He realised that he was not afraid of the man anymore, but he did not wish to cause any futher upset. There wasn't a sound inside the chalet. The sound of clothes flapping on the line behind him, startled him for a moment. Woman's clothes. Underclothing. The boy wondered at the woman his father kept. At the heart she must have and the stories told of her. Somebody in school had said that her husband had come in from Kilkenny one night and set upon his father in a pub. There had been a trail of blood along the pavement outside. But he did not believe the whole story. His father could watch over himself well enough. He had reached the rear window of the chalet. The curtains had not been pulled. He would be able to look into the cramped bedroom without being seen. The cat by the oak tree told his presence, but he ignored it. Then he was moving again, wary of foot, towards the window. And his father's face came to mind once more and he thought to turn and run. A memory: one sunny afternoon. Dangling from the low beams in the barn. His father's footsteps by the barn door. His name being called. Curses.

—Making a stukawn of me in front of the whole place. You won't ever do it again, me bucko. And I'll guarantee you that!

Swinging high from the rafters. The belt flailing about his legs. Afraid to let go in case the man would beat him about the head. The buckle catching him on the thighs. The tears in his eyes. His legs dancing to escape the stinging belt.

—Will you ever do it again?

—No, daddy, never!

—Never?

—I swear to you I won't!

Then his grip suddenly failing on the beam. The man's boot in his side. The man shaking him and the beast that was in his eyes.

He saw the woman and the blood that had congealed about her right shoulder on the scruffy bed-linen. He heard a low, animal-like moaning. As if hot irons had been taken to her very soul in order to spark some life into her bleached body. A deep, primitive moan of bewilderment. A dress had been thrown on the floor beside the bed. The flowery blouse she wore. The dark, damp hair of her thighs under the gussetting of her knickers. There was neither sight nor sign of the man. He stepped down from his position on the wooden crate and circled the chalet again. He would have to go in by the front door. The cat sat, sunning her person by the concrete-block steps. He drove the animal aside with a wave of his hand as he entered. He stood inside the door and watched his father. His sleeping figure cast carelessly across the pull-down table. In suit and tie. The contentment of the just upon his face. The boy turned sharply when the woman's groaning caught his ear again. She was moving her free arm as if to signal her distress. His father would not wake so easily, he knew. He had seen the man in such a slumber many times before. For a moment he hesitated. Then he approached the figure on the bed and drew the blanket up over her thighs. The gun lay where it had fallen, on the floor beside the sink unit. He lifted it up carefully and re-set the safety catch once more. Then he lay the gun upon the bed and, keeping a distant eye on the far end of the chalet, whispered a convulsed prayer into the woman's ear. He felt easy in the wisdom that, if the man should wake suddenly and turn his temper on him, he would set the gun on his father without scruple. When he had rounded off the mumbled prayer and assured himself that he could do little for the woman but summon help, he took up the shotgun and made for the door. He thought he noticed the man shift in his sleep. He broke the gun just to assure himself that the second barrel had not been loosed on the woman. Standing by the door, he stared down absently at the dozing man, as if goading him into waking. Eyeing his father as he would a waking man, he spat onto the muddied lino under his feet.

—You're only a filthy pig! That's all you are!

Then he broke the gun again and made off across the fields for the house.

Margaret could miss school and look after the shop until she came back. She would keep an eye on the child too. The others would be off out the door shortly anyway. The woman kept her eye on the fields from the gable window, but she could see nothing. It couldn't have taken him that long. She would have to go down herself and see. By the laneway across the tannery fields to the chalet itself. As she listened to the chatter of the children at the breakfast table, she drove from her mind the dark thoughts which assailed her. An image: the boy and the man struggling together while the woman slept. The dogs were barking again. She went out into the yard with the child and crossed to the gate. She decided that she would wait no longer. Going back into the house, she gave instructions for the child to be dressed and for the shop to be opened in good time for the factory. A man's voice, clear and comforting, was giving out good weather on the radio as she closed the door behind her. She could hear the voice of her eldest daughter ordering all as she passed out of the yard. Out on the laneway she forgot the family and considered the man ahead of her. How he could still touch her when half a mile away at the end of the field. She knew that she would take a knife to him if he ever again crossed one of the children. And she wondered why she had sought to sacrifice her eldest son that morning. Voices over the years. Voices offering their own peculiar comfort and consolation in her grief. When the man had first shown his nature.

—Sure he comes home to you, doesn't he? At least you have that much.

Early morning arguments. Problems with the shop and money. The tongues at her again, whenever the man attempted to rest for a few months. She marked how they would only comment when he had turned once more for comfort to the measure. As if each had been waiting for the man to fall again. Relief in their eyes when he did tumble. Glee, by cunning, transmuted into concern.

—Sure you mustn't know from one day to the next with him.

She paused a moment to brush away the dust of the morning from her dress. The day would indeed be a warm one. The voice on the radio had reason for once. That time she had strolled down the laneway when she was carrying the youngest child. A thing she had never done before. To walk out into the fields and forget the house and the shop. The contentment it afforded her. The soft distance from the frantic dealings of the day. When all the voices told her of her son's distracted ways and the troubles he constantly courted.

—He'll turn out just like him. If you don't watch him.

There was a figure in the distance, at the point where the lane met the tannery fields. But she could make out neither the face nor the bearing of the stranger. It might have been either man. She stood back in towards the ditch as the walker approached. The gun cradled on his forearm. The figure appeared to be limping. She knew that it must be her son, but still she did not call out to the man.

He had hurt his knee crossing the stile. Day-dreaming. Some odd notion that had taken him, to make off down by the furze near the ballast-pit to take a rabbit. Or perhaps even a fox. Realising how high the sun stood, he dismissed the idea for what it was. The image of the woman was before his eyes too. A bloodied ikon on his memory. The man slumbering on the fold-down table. He would be asleep when the guards arrived. The woman might still be alive. He thought he noticed something further up the lane. As though someone had suddenly hidden themselves from his view. It could not be the man. Had his father sought to head him off, surely he would have made for the house? He carried on. In any event, he told himself, he had the gun in his hand. He glanced upwards as he walked. Towards the screeching creatures above his head. Towards the swifts, their scimitar wings scything the air. Tumbling and turning in their flight without fear. High in the air, taking hapless insects on the wing. Something his father had told him once. Swifts and swallows. The higher they fly, the hotter it will be. And how to watch for the end of winter and the coming of the flowers and bushes and how to tell false spring. Only once had they ever gone out shooting together. It had been down by the ballast-pit. With the banks and the maybushes and all.

They approach one another slowly. Both keep in towards the ditch. The air is heavy with the reek of rhododendron run wild.

—If her, then her dress. Was it green or red?

Sound of feet shuffling on gravel, of switches snapping at faces.

—If Tom, then he'll stoop as he walks. Got that from me.

The thrumming of a hundred scattered swarms of bees frames the silence.

—If my father, then I'll point the gun at him. Shout stop! Stop!

Neither one knows the name of the other. Are you my mother? Are you father? Are you son?

—If Tom, mustn't rise my hand. Think I have a weapon. Might shoot. If him, then take to my heels. Warn the children.

They might only guess as they move circumspectly through the dust of the pock-marked lane.

—Guards never touch me. If I shot him. Say he attacked me.

At a crook in the lane, sun striking both blind, they shout together as one.

—Come out! Come out! Come out, I said!

—Jesus! Jesus! Tom, it's me!

The woman was standing in the middle of the lane now, smiling at him. Telling him to mind the gun and asking him if he was alright. The bright yellow dress and the light summer jacket she had thrown over her shoulders.

—Did he hurt her, Tom?

Her arms were around him and he was crying. She gave him a coarse handkerchief to dry his tears. The sun had lost its early cloud now and they could both feel the warmth on their faces as they made their way back up the lane. The boy was telling her about what he had seen. The awful quiet about the chalet and the woman on the bed. His father senseless in another corner. He wanted to tell her about the cat which had kept appearing in his path. How it followed him to the laneway, as if for luck. But he felt that his mother might rebuke him for his foolishness. The woman noticed the way the old stammer had wound its way in among the boy's words again. The way his speech was thrown whenever turmoil or upset threatened. He ran ahead of her, as she had asked, to 'phone the barracks. She watched the boy disappear in by the gate, pausing a moment to retrieve the brass-bottomed cartridge from the shotgun. Then she slipped it into her jacket and carried on.

When she reached the house, she found her son waiting in the hall with the sergeant, a stout impatient man. Two guards had already been sent down along the river to the chalet. When the man in the uniform left, bearing the gun inelegantly across his forearm, the woman crossed the hall with her eldest children to the room they called the Africa room. She smiled a moment at the innocence of the conceit. For the family scarcely used the Africa room at all. With its heavily upholstered suite and the embossed wallpaper, there was something too sombre about the room for everyday use. A clumsy carving of a lioness stood upon the mantlepiece. The work of white hands. The glass case by the door held a pair of ornamental drums. Various ebony fashionings, a piece of ivory set in stone and some dogeared photographs betokened the sojourn in a hot climate of a middle-aged priest. The room seemed to the woman at times, to be little more than a museum to the memory of a brother-in-law who had died on the missions in Angola. Slipping off her canvas shoes, she ran the tip of her bare foot over a floral pattern in the dark face of the carpet. Africa must be like this, she felt. Red, oppressive, sultry. Or perhaps it was more like the sky outside. Azure, expansive, joyous. Who was to know? Sitting opposite her on the settee, her son toyed with his thumbs as he joked. His laughter was that of a child, uncertain of the matter of a joke he had stumbled upon in the company of his elders. A memory of carrying him strayed across the path of the woman's thoughts. big with the boy, standing in the yard, throwing scraps to the fowl. Not knowing who was in her. Was it man? Was it woman? As she had not known who he was when he had approached her on the lane a short while before. She had sung to him then, sung a song to the nestling in her belly. Softly, lest someone might hear her and shame take the good from it. A secret between herself and a nameless one, from a time when there was no memory.

She looked up from the ruddy frieze of the carpet and demanded that a kettle be put on. Water must be boiled. Her voice was coarse in its authority. And would he ever check on the others. They heard the boy's footsteps fade along the hall. The woman looked at her daughter. She wanted to touch her. Woman touch woman. The way she mustn't touch her son. For sons must not come too close.

—What did I go sending him out for at all, Margaret?

—You done right, mam. You done right, so you did.

The woman in the yellow print dress sought to call herself to counsel now. Why had she sought to sacrifice her son? Was there some evil that had made her send him forth to fight his own father in her name? Wasn't that what she had done? Margaret, her eldest daughter, was kneeling beside her now. The women smiled for one another. They could hear the others in the hallway. The boy's voice calling for a teapot. For a moment, neither of them spoke. The younger woman rested her hands gently upon her mother's head, in the attitude of one invoking a blessing. When she finally spoke, she was firm with the woman, after the fashion of a mother with a frightened child.

—You done right, so you did. You done the right thing, mam.

And the women cried together quietly and, in the fullness of the moment, were content.

Elgin Avenue

AFTER SPENDING A COUPLE OF DAYS with friends in a council flat down the road, they both returned to the house on Elgin Avenue. Eoin followed the girl up the dark stairs, past the dog-dirt and newspapers, into their room. They found it much as they had left it, although the padlock on the door had been forced in their absence. He lay down on the mattress in the corner, watching her as she went about sorting through her effects. The satchel slung over her shoulder. The heavy jumper she wore to mask her slight frame. A black hat sat jauntily upon her head. Plaits and bows. If he lay in under the blankets, she might start to annoy him about his sleeping habits. He saw her run her hand through her hair as she stood before the window. Noises he knew well, made their moment upon his ears. Pots being moved about in the flat below them. A radio chirping away harmlessly in the distance. Voices conspiring together in other rooms. Music seeping through from the basement flat. Then sleep, into which he crept quietly, as a child who is taken in a sulk.

—Theresa! Theresa!

His own voice drew him back to wakefulness. She was kneeling by the bed, talking softly. But not to him. Eoin looked up at the figure standing by the door. The Newry man from the back flat eyed him. The one who lived alone. His face pock-marked as a result of being set upon in a pub at home. They had seldom spoken, although they passed one another regularly enough on the stairs. He had called to tell them that there had been no trouble since Simon's death. That it was safe enough to sleep in the house again. He told Eoin of the well-dressed stranger who had called and demanded to see him. The tall man had gone about from room to room, lifting up pillows and checking the fly-leaves of books in search of a name. When someone tackled him, the intruder went into a rage. Swearing and drawing down abuse on everyone, he insisted that Eoin be told on his return to contact his family immediately. From the telling, Eoin recognised the features of his father's brother. When he spoke with his own brother on the phone that evening, he found, as he had suspected, that his father had suffered a fresh heart attack. The coldness of his brother's voice on the line. The sombre cut of his words. His grandmother would be listening in the parlour. When his brother left down the receiver, she would call out across the evening silence.

—Was that who I think it was?

—It was Eoin, Gran.

—And what did your brother have to say for himself, tell us?

His father had been buried the previous Monday. Looking out at Theresa from the telephone box, he realised that there was nowhere he might be left alone to cry quietly. He called the girl.

They passed the rest of the evening in a pub near the station. They laughed together over the squat, wondering when the bookie who owned the block would finally decide to pull down each house. Whenever his tongue sought to name his father's name, he drew back at the last moment, fearing the cold censure of the girl's silence. He found himself, as the drink took his thoughts, speculating on whether he might break with London altogether on his return home. They spoke of Simon's death in the squat and of the police. He had lost himself, for a moment, in a quiet telling of the dead men's faces, when she turned to him. The noise of the juke-box in the corner baffled her words at first. He leaned closer to her. Smell of sleeping in her standing clothes. Low, north London tongue with shades of squatter's jargon thrown in. Eyes which charmed the light and measured with design. Her hands reached for the cigarette.

—Would you like to take me with you, Eoin?

He looked away. Towards the bar and the tight-bellied

youths. Their cocksure manner. Smooth-lipped sensuality. The soft aggressiveness they displayed towards one another. Their ordered lives, he considered. Work, drink, copulation, sleep. He turned back sourly to the girl again. She was giving him time now. He knew that. Teasing out his drunken dignity until, in mute submission, he would finally relent. An image of his grandmother came to him. The big widow sitting in her astute silence by the fire. His father at the kitchen table. A lukewarm mug of tea in his hands. The old woman smiling to herself, when her son finally agreed to second some small scheme or other. Words bartered cutely to save two hearts.

They slept badly in the squat that night. Eoin rose a number of times in the dark hours to be sick down in the toilet on the first return. As he crouched over a bowl, the constant grumble of the traffic along the avenue was a sort of distraction. When his stomach had settled, he sat himself in an armchair by the window and smoked. It seemed only a moment before the quiet of the young day had moved him unwittingly to reflection. His eyes fixed themselves on the new high-rise block across the road. Clean, functional, pre-cast concrete units. Suddenly, the man was before him: he who fathered me. Poor, luckless bastard. Who passed his time in this great town. The forties. Younger son on a small farm. The boat, then the train. A lodging house up in Harlesden, the shortest hop from the railway. A woman at home you courted. My mother. Sick woman. Consumption. A grandmother's voice saying, 'Never mention it! Sounds bad!' For the seed and the stock. Oh, Jesus, I'm sorry. I am sorry. Why could I never speak, write, smile even? That I begrudged you even the smallest unlit corner of my life. Now, it is too late. It is always too late. Jesus! Jesus! Jesus!

He slept fitfully in the armchair, wrapped in a tartan quilt, away from the warmth and succour of the woman in the bed. He remembered half-waking a number of times to the sound of someone hammering on the door below. Demented screams. A guttural accent roaring profanities for all the world to hear. When they rose, they stepped over a threshold bespattered with blood, where a man, driven wild by a mixture of amphetamines and alcohol, had battered himself unconscious against the front door. Theresa laughing, as they carried their bags down the road.

—You didn't hear him shouting, 'I'm the madman of the Harrow Road!', did you? All night he was at it. Scottish bastard. Hope he's done hisself in and all.

They crossed water. Dublin was wet. They stayed with some friends in a crowded flat on Palmerston Road. Because of the bus strike, they walked everywhere. They spoke with one another as if they had just met. Theresa told of her family and the flat up in Ealing. They laughed together at the little vanities of brothers and sisters. Her accent seemed less caustic to his ear now. A London working-class accent, tinged with the transatlantic mouthings she had gleaned from those about her in the squat. She would survive, he knew, where some in the house would not. The sober humour of her way would keep her at a clear distance from the rougher edge of things and the needle. Sometimes she frightened and appalled Eoin.

—My dad comes back in one night and starts calling me a whore. And he goes and hits me mum. Next day, I was gone.

The tale of her mother. Slow-witted woman, bruised by the constant turmoil of her life. Another glimpse: Theresa a child, watching for that hour of evening when her father would leave the flat to visit another woman on the floor above them. Her mother turning her head towards the window, to feign ignorance or indifference. Sometimes she paid a brief visit to her mother's flat. With her father gone and her siblings scattered to the city, there was a sort of peace. Her mother, sullen-faced, sitting alone in the gloomy living-room. A television chanting away to itself in the corner. Theresa drew upon her cigarette. She was laughing.

—I learned to tell the time very young, see. Every time me old dad had a hard-on, I sussed it must be around seven, or thereabouts.

He was surprised that Theresa did not wish to know

more of the house she was to visit. He had told her much over the previous months, of course. Of his two brothers. One tied by primogeniture and pig-headedness to the land. The other studying in the regional tech. A sister married with a national teacher in Galway city. And his mother, who had passed the days since the funeral with his sister. He told Theresa of his uncle Matt, an accountant in Athlone, who kept a distant eye on all matters relating to the farm. The same man who had scoured the squat in London, to carry to Eoin the news of his father's death. He told of his grandmother, the very hand which had always guided the house both in sickness and in health. Theresa did not ask on. On a cold Monday morning, they left Dublin. They were picked up almost as soon as they left the city bus in Maynooth. Outside Ballinasloe, they took a lift from a commercial traveller to the village. Past hedgerows with berries. The nearer they drew, the more familiar became the landmarks. A roadside shrine near the crossroads. The low stone wall which skirted the cemetery. Black and Tans story, he told her. Lot made of a little incident. They walked out from the village, past the school. By children streaming from the playground. He listened as they passed, to their songs. Songs, consumer songs, he told himself. And all the terrible prattle about independence. He would not visit his father's grave today. Perhaps later on in the week, when the idea of the man's passing became easier to understand. He must lie to his grandmother. They took the road for Tulla. The weak light beating its way through the trees. The mottled shroud of lately-fallen leaves. The very air itself, told Eoin that autumn was upon them. He noted in himself, that same sense of betrayal he had ever felt as a boy, when the fresh chill of the mornings presaged the imminent return to boarding school.

At the foot of the long lane which led up to the house Theresa drew back, as if in sudden apprehension. When he had reassured her, they took up their haversacks once more. From the head of the lane, they could see an elderly woman hunting a lone cow into the byre. A tall woman, dressed in heavy dungarees with a red scarf tied about her head. She called out to them as they passed and gestured towards the farmhouse. Theresa watched, as the woman brought a great thorny switch down upon the beast's back. Then she turned away and followed Eoin slowly into the house. A red-haired youth in overalls looked up from his newspaper as they entered. A mug of tea in one hand. Theresa nodded towards the stranger. He winked at her. A dog lay sleeping at his feet. Before the range a cat, stretched snug, watched the intruders.

—Well, Eoinín!

—How are you, Fergus?

—The prodigal son. Are you not going to offer that poor girl there a seat at all?

Theresa sat to one side. Everything about the kitchen set her on edge. The stone floor, the clothes drying over the range, the animals sleeping near the table. She chose not to interrupt the conversation, even when the youngest brother Michael appeared in the kitchen. The sniping tone of their words told of an intimacy which she had never known. When the old woman arrived in, there was silence for a moment. Leaving the bucket with the chicken scraps in the porch, she went to wash her hands in the kitchen sink. She peered over her shoulder to speak to them. Theresa found it difficult to meet the eyes which moved over her. She stumbled when she spoke, acutely aware of the sharpness of her accent on the air. She watched the tall woman. The wisp of grey hair jutting out from under the scarf. The long, sinewy hands which told of no sore ageing. The woman smiled down at her.

—We didn't realise that Eoin would be bringing anyone with him.

—I didn't think of it on the 'phone.

—No. Well, anyway, there's always the fold-down in the front room. Theresa, wasn't it?

The following morning, with Fergus and Michael, he drove into Galway to visit his mother. Theresa stayed behind on the advice of his grandmother. The three scarcely spoke on the way. They passed Merlin Park Hospital in the city. Eoin considered its sister houses scattered throughout the country. His mother, lying silent in a darkened room all those years ago. First one lung to be collapsed, then the other. Thinking on a man who had jilted her, when she entered the sanatorium, for a fresher girl. His father cycling in to visit her from the farm, every weekend. A sick-bed courtship. In the housing estate where his sister lived, Eoin was struck by the numbers of children on the streets and by the absence of older people. He smiled at his sister as they entered the house, marking the signs of the new suburbs both in her dress and in her speech. They were led into the sitting-room. Soft carpets, a copy of *Cosmopolitan* on the table. A large woollen donkey, brought back from some holiday in Spain. Their mother joined them a few moments later. It was obvious to all that the woman was under the stupefying spell of some sedative or other. They followed her sluggish movements as she sat before them. When his brothers excused themselves to go into town, Eoin was left alone with the two women. Now and then, his sister would pass some comment as if to make him suffer, in some oblique way, for his waywardness. He realised that somehow the cloying cleanliness and the stifling order of the house best suited his mother's needs for the present. He watched his sister as she returned from the kitchen with coffee. How the fat had begun to lodge contentedly on her hips. The measured gait betraying a slight unease with her surroundings. When her husband appeared a while later, he was ushered into the kitchen with scarcely a comment.

He was alone before his mother now, without a word his tongue might catch onto or a soft comment he could muster. He looked up at her. The dark rings around her eyes from crying. The suit she wore, a gaudy mourning-dress. Countrywoman's clothes. He wanted to stretch out his hand to her, to take her hand in his. But he could not. Grieved to find that he was at a loss as to how he might comfort his mother, he turned away from her. She was crying now, dabbing her tears with a crumpled handkerchief which reeked of lavender. Sobbing, nodding her head from side to side.

—We had no way of getting in touch with you, Eoin. Matt had to go over. You know that, don't you?

—I know that, Mam. I know that.

—Only that he found that address through the pub …

He railed at the mention of his uncle's name. The thought of the man, blustering his way about the house on Elgin Avenue. Leaning against a door. Forcing a padlock. Lifting a pillow. Matt and his grandmother drawing up battle-lines together. His mother leaned forward, almost whispering now.

—You're not in any trouble, are you? Eoin?

They stopped off in the village on the way home. The pub was full. Eoin sat in a corner with Michael, while Fergus joined in a game of darts at the far end of the bar. When Michael spoke of his mother, there was little warmth in his words. He spoke of her as one who had always appeared on the brink of one collapse or another. Eoin regarded the red-headed figure by the dartboard. For a brief moment, he sensed envy well up in him at his brother's easy manner with those around him. The soft turn of his words when disputing one point or another. The one who had not been sent off to boarding school. He and Michael remained together, at a distance from the crowd, until closing-time. It was almost midnight by the time they arrived back at the house. A light was burning in the kitchen. They found the old woman sitting by the range, listening with a half-ear to the late news on the wireless. She turned to greet them.

—What kept you till this hour?

—We stopped off in Walsh's.

—Isn't it well for you, all the same.

Fergus threw his coat on the chair and made for bed. The old woman reached for her book as she stood up.

—That girl's gone down, Eoin. She said she was tired. I don't know at all.

He sat for a while with Michael, before the last of the fire and, when they had both run their sullen thoughts to ground together, lay down on the sofa in his long coat and fell to sleep.

His grandmother asked him to do the milking with Fergus over the following week. It would give Michael time to study for the autumn repeats. Each morning now, he would be roused by his brother. The coarse, red hair and the half-shaven face leaning over him on the fold-down bed.

—Up, you lazy hippy!

Theresa never rose before noon. She told Eoin that she feared the company of his grandmother. They went for walks together in the afternoon. He would tell her a little of the order of the land and the farms about. But she showed no wonder. Nothing seemed to touch her heart. Eoin recalled that even Simon's death in the squat had been little more than an awkward experience for her. They spoke of the night only once. As though the man's passing were merely an odd turn of memory. He found that he could not dismiss the night as easily himself. The frantic shouts at the door as they lay abed. Then the scene in Simon's flat. A dark-haired girl walking him up and down the floor. Someone else forcing him to drink scalding coffee. They seemed to have scarcely returned to their beds when the first scream rent the silence. Eoin remembered walking the length of Elgin Avenue to find a phone. The odd, dazed creatures of the early morning on the streets. Their eyes on him, querying. Then, in the wake of the ambulance men, uniformed police. When the intruders had all quit the house, they were left in the dead man's flat with the others. There were people smoking, there was music somewhere in the background. Arms around the woman who had just lost her man. As she rocked back and forth, arms around her. Shrewd, heartless words of comfort. Someone came upon a hat which had been left behind by one of the policemen. A girl danced with it on her head. They took turns at playing charades with the hat. Theresa, in the corner of Eoin's eye, sitting with the weeping woman. When someone suggested that the hat might have been left as a ruse, they all scattered to their separate rooms. Only the sound of the woman keening below in the basement disturbed their sleep.

It was when Eoin was left to himself that his father's voice came tripping after him. In those moments when silence stole up unexpectedly. Down by the barn, when he was hunting the cows out after the evening milking. How his father had paused, a small man with a crooked cap struggling for breath, to talk to him.

—You know too much, Eoin. That's your problem. You can be told nothing.

Or at night, when he was before the range. That odd habit his father had of chewing his lip as he mused to himself. His grandmother stalking the silence behind him. Then, that morning when his father was crushed against the gable wall of the milking parlour by a nervous beast. Little children, they were then. Tears and upset when they saw the labourer helping him to the door. The doctor and the long drive to hospital. And his grandmother taking over the house until his father came out of hospital again.

He spoke with his uncle Matt on the 'phone. His uncle would call out the following Sunday. He was looking forward to their meeting, his uncle said. And who was the young girl? He must have an eye for the pretty women, like his father before him. His uncle's voice grated. The soft, smug tones and the unctious camaraderie. Eoin smiled at his own image of the man behind the voice. The heavy belly of the celibate, the puckering of the lips to feign concern. He had always found it hard to countenance the idea that his father was related to the man at all. They would all have a late dinner on the Sunday then, his grandmother declared. It would suit his uncle best. The man's unwelcome shadow hung over the following days.

The dark and the slighting cold of the early mornings threw him too. The familiar sounds and fresh smells. All that was dew-damp and masked in silence. He longed in a way, though, for the false ease of life in the house on Elgin Avenue. For the company of those without name. The senseless passage of the days. Dreams and half-dreams and living off distilled memories. Theresa beside him in careless sleep. Easy rutting on the early morning. They walked into the village together a number of times. In the corner of the grocer's, they would sit and drink, far from the ears of those his father would have shunned on the streets. They talked of London and the people in the house. A couple from Wales, who worked all the hours of the day and night to buy a cottage on the coast somewhere. The three students who shared the back flat. The man from Newry and how he would wake to a pillow spotted with blood. Something about the septum of the nose and cocaine. They recalled the only other time they had been bothered by the police. It was after the Tower bombing. The door thrown open by a Special Branch man. They were all questioned about a couple of strays from Belfast who had spent a night there some weeks before.

—Irish too, are you son?

That pulse of resentment, which he had strained to banish from his heart over the following weeks. Theresa had simply sworn at them. In his father's house, he had little to say to either of his brothers. Sometimes, his grandmother would stop him suddenly and throw him with a question. It might be about his future plans or about his life in London. He sought to be vague with her. But there was no peace at any turn, until he had divested himself of some notion which satisfied her. It awed him to find that Theresa was easier in the company of his own family than he. Her indifference to the ebb and flow of their lives left her content to observe the smaller things. The way his grandmother had of scouring the pans with salt. Or her habit of talking to herself as she listened to the news on the radio. She was settled enough in herself to offer the old woman help with the household chores. In the company of his brother Fergus, Eoin felt the new course of the family. There was one morning on which his resentment almost moved him to strike the smiling face. A light drizzle, as he tramped behind his brother towards the milking parlour. Across the grey concrete of the haggard, their boots singing out their progress in the dawn. There was a problem with the cooler and Fergus cursed as he bent to investigate. They tried to avoid one another. Something his brother muttered about the new future in milk. The regular cheque. He was only half-listening to the words. Then the twist in tone, all of a sudden.

—Tell us anyway ... where did you pick that one up from? If you don't mind my asking, that is.

—How do you mean?

—Her. Theresa. I'd say she's well used to the three-point turn. Practice, of course.

—Are you trying to say something to me, Fergus?

They could both hear the old woman calling them for breakfast. Then, the voice telling their names in turn. The sound of the dogs running before her. He left down the suction bottles and faced his brother. They read one another by the eyes. Their grandmother was crossing the haggard. Her words told them that she sensed she was being ignored. Fergus laid his hand on his brother's shoulder. His face inched closer. The terrier was at the door, snapping at the heels of a cow. Eoin pushed his brother's hand away in anger. Fergus was standing now, gazing down on him.

—You're not the blue-eyed boy here anymore, Eoin. That day's dead and gone.

Pattern day fell on the Sunday. There would be the usual dressing of the graves and the show in the marquee field. None of the family would visit the graves this year however. It would be too soon after the recent death. Eoin's grandmother was to go up to a neighbour's house for the afternoon. All was to be ready for the evening meal, when his uncle drove in from Athlone. His grandmother called to him, before leaving in the car with Fergus. He must have the roast on early and have the place in order by the time they returned. The girl could lend a hand too. When he heard the car pass down the lane-way, he fell back to sleep. He woke to Theresa standing over him. But she would not lie in. They ate a quiet breakfast. When they heard Michael rising, they left the house for a walk. There were bells on the air. Distant sounds. A crow-scarer firing erratically. They wandered up towards the high fields. The sounds of horns and recorded music. The show, he told her. For the Pattern. From the high fields, they could look across the land and see the features of the village scored into the face of the fields. The water tower of the national school and the church spire. The awkward mass of the old workhouse set to one side. Theresa was talking about his grandmother. Something about teaching her to bake soda bread. He thought of his father, standing outside the church gates talking to another farmer. Their laughter cut into him. His father flicked the butt of a cigarette onto the ground. Theresa crossed into the orchard ahead of him. She ran her hands along the lichen-shrouded limbs. It was a notion, he explained to her, which his mother had taken. She had tended to the orchard for a time, then let it settle back into nature when she tired of it. Not like his father, he told her. Solid, consistent, silent. She ran through the trees, teasing him to catch her. When he caught up with her, they stood as one. Then, the upset struck. The whole moment of the thing chilling his heart. He was sobbing, unburdening himself of the memory. When it had passed, they walked on together in silence. They crossed into the haggard. Hearing Michael in the house, he drew her aside and nodded towards the steps leading up to the loft. In a corner of the great room, they lay down together. Must of oats and barley, must of woman. Seed thrown, barren where it fell. When they came to rest, he knew her for one who would surely pass from his life. A sudden and unspoken jealousy took him. A jealousy of those, whom he had never met, who would lie with her after him. By the time they had crossed to the house again, the idea had lost itself among a thousand others.

The pheasant-pattern crockery had not been used since the Christmas before. The table was moved into the middle of the floor and the dogs were kept outside. Eoin drew the cork on the first bottle, while Fergus stood to carve the roast. His uncle was at the head of the table, with his back to the range. They sat to eat. The talk ran as it would. There was mention of some of the new grants. Had Fergus got all the details yet? His uncle knew just the man who could help him there. It was quite simply a matter of information and timing. His grandmother interrupted.

—Did you hear about Cassidys over beyond, Matt?

—I know the man who's dealing with the case, sure. Three men and a dog. You can't run a farm like that these days.

—And what will happen so?

—Well, there's a civil bill out from the tax crowd anyway. And, I suppose, they must owe the banks a few bob too.

—And will they lose the farm?

—They might well.

Occasionally, Theresa was drawn into the conversation. She was questioned about her background. There was talk of London and cities in general. They had all done their stint in London, Eoin's uncle told her. A few years among the Irish of the roads. There was no choice then, of course. He offered her more wine. There was a second bottle. His uncle told jokes.

—Says the black lad to Paddy, 'For God's sake don't tell the Jewboy it's Christmas or we're bunched altogether!'

He leaned across the table to tell a tale to the men, of a prostitute in Cork. His face struck a separate attitude for each ridge and furrow in the tale. He banged the table with his fist to sustain their laughter. The old woman affected to be shocked. She told Theresa that she had no time for men's talk. Eoin could hear his grandmother in conversation with Theresa. Their easy banter teased his temper. Fergus was arranging for his uncle to sort out the books as soon as possible. Only himself and Michael seemed to be on the perimeter of things.

—And how long are you planning on staying, Eoin?

—Not too long.

—You're in no hurry. I suppose.

His uncle turned back to Fergus again. Eoin lit a cigarette and sat back to watch them. There was nothing now. There was nothing at all. Of that he was sure. Words which trailed his every thought: there is no home now. A yearning took him, for the sanctuary of London and a house where people came and went, scarcely knowing one another's names. Where hurt was not possible in the way of things. He considered the two men who had died recently. His father, shy and diffident, stealing away at the bidding of the fresh season. He watched Fergus, his father's shadow on earth now, and he considered the dead man in London. The mannerisms of the culture in which he had resided. Sat inside a darkened room with his girl-friend. A syringe and tourniquet by their bedside. His name slipping away forever, unmarked by the houses around. They were talking around him now. Laughing about one of the dogs. His grandmother cast her head back in mock despair.

—A bit of a *mí-ádh* is what he is. No earthly use to anyone. And you go steady on that wine there, Matthew. You have to drive home, remember.

His grandmother rose to go to bed. Fergus and Michael went off to tidy up for a dance. He watched the old woman leave aside her speckled apron. There was something in the way she turned to them, which reminded him of his father. The sternness of her smile. His uncle poured for him. They had drunk both bottles down to the very lees now and Theresa wanted to retire. He would be left alone with uncle and two glasses. He walked her down the corridor and kissed her gently on the forehead before returning to the kitchen. The man had pulled his chair over to the range. With the short poker, he raked the ashes, then rested his legs on the old butter box which served as a fuel bin. From the table, Eoin watched his uncle sip his share. The way he had of picking at his teeth after a meal. He inclined his head towards Eoin. With the wine, his eyes had lost their usual lustre. He brushed a shadow from the crease of his trousers.

—You know, there's always a welcome here for you. It is your home after all.

The dogs were barking out in the haggard. Perhaps a fox had strayed in from the fields, the man by the range suggested. There was no reply from the figure at the table.

There was no fear of them catching a fox, his uncle continued. They were too well-fed for that. You had to keep them hungry, like cats. There was once a chap down by the commons one time, and he had this gorgeous-looking, Persian blue. Well now, it was really a show cat. Competitions and all of that. But, by God, it was the best ratter for miles around. Big, furry, blue lad, for all the world like a little fecking poodle.

—Wasn't Fergus man enough to tell me himself?

—What?

—I said, could Fergus not do the dirty work. How well he couldn't tell me himself.

His uncle drew his legs down off the butter box. Stooping, he picked up the empty glass and left it down on the table. Impatiently, he brushed a few imaginary crumbs from his jumper. He rested his hands on the table and looked down on the younger man. For a moment, it seemed that one man might strike the other. The older man's eyes were heavy with drink. He drew himself unsteadily to his full height.

—Don't push it, Eoin. Alright?

—Couldn't he have told me himself, I asked you?

—Look, you weren't here when you were wanted, sonny Jim. That's my last word on it. Just … just don't push it. Eoin. Alright?

Now, his uncle was putting on his overcoat. He was fumbling about for the keys he had mislaid. They were in the pocket of his waistcoat. And Eoin must call out to see his mother at least once before he went back. He could bring the girl too, if he wanted. When he looked up from his glass, his uncle had already left the kitchen. He could hear him bidding a goodnight to his grandmother. Then the man was gone and the sound of the motor died along the lane leading down by the far fields. A bitterness began to well up in his heart, for what might have been. He called to mind the immediate world without the kitchen. The chilled autumnal dark in which the fields lay shrouded. The creatures of the frozen gloom, who scurried about from drain to drain. For a while, he thought that his heart would get the better of him and that he would indeed stumble down towards the bedroom to strike the girl in vengeance. Then, just as swiftly, all rashness went from him and he was left wordless in a backwash of remorse. Against the ticking of the clock above his head, there was only the sound of his own sobbing now and his grandmother's keen voice, calling him to check the range, bolt all the doors and quench the kitchen lights before retiring.

The Doppler Effect

THERE WAS INCENSE TOO, carried across the body of the church by the sharp breeze which gusted in from the quays and the river. The old women who sat aloof in the side aisles were watching them. The children sang together as one warm voice. An infant cried and was hushed. They were only half-listening to the words of the parish priest before them. A woman was shouting outside in the street. Her words coming shrill and keen against the softer tones of the man in the pulpit. A child giggled and a hand was laid firmly on her shoulder. They watched the bishop strike the stage, noting the soft hands which set the great domed hat upon his head. The parish priest who bore away the crozier. His hushed footsteps on the altar carpet. A truck shuddered by along the alley-way. The old women were listening fast now. The bishop was speaking about the pledge, but his words were lost to the boy.

His eyes wandered. He sought to sum all the colours he could see about him. The walls, the marbled columns along the centre aisle. The cold face of the pulpit. Stark tones fading into pastels. But his mother would not look to her left, nor would she look to her right. He thought to number the niches in the vaulted ceiling above. Then the odd octagonal designs on the transept wall. The statue of Saint Damien itself, which changed aspect as you moved from one side to the other. The children grew restless in their seats. In the massive stained-glass windows which fronted onto the street, the light died as clouds scurried to hide the face of the sun. The boy glanced across the aisles again. But his mother would not look to her left, nor would she look to her right. He stood up slowly with the others to join in the hymn.

—Praise to the Holiest in the High

And in the depth be praise
In all his words most wonderful
Most sure in all his ways.

There was a girl in the front row. Her skin he would touch. Her father standing solid among the other parents. His skin. It is soft and it is dark too. Like her skin. Because he is her father.

—And in the garden secretly

Someone who changed-over had written that song, the parish priest told them.

—And on the cross on high

A sort of Protestant. But he changed before he died.

—Should teach his brethren and inspire

Another song he wrote too. They had sung it when they were all drowning on the Titanic.

—To suffer and to die.

Or he was drowning or he wrote it. The bishop was smiling down on them. He was talking about when he was a boy. When the bishop was a boy. Two girls whispered to one another in front of him. The soft stuff of their dresses. One has crimped hair, the other ringlets, like her mother. There was a commotion by the doors leading onto the quays. A small, unwashed child and a large, unkempt labrador had wandered in. The bishop smiled and raised his hands as if to invite the congregation to share in the joke. The parish priest hurried down the altar steps without genuflecting and led both the hang-jowled dog and the child out once more into the street. A man laughed in the gathering and his wife nudged him. But his own mother turned neither to her left nor to her right. As if she would not see. The bishop carried on. The soft folds of his face. The eyes which did not bully. A teacher genuflected, then slipped out by the alley-way door to oversee the preparation of the teas. The bishop laughed at something he had said himself. A woman smiled to her man. The children shifted in their seats. A girl, with no name for her father, was silent in the front pew. Seagulls called to one another over the river, as they banked off down towards the station.

The boy fingered the medallion pinned to his jacket. A dove, light streaming from its sacred head. He inclined his gaze towards the side confessionals. He saw his mother, her eyes steady on the brightly-garbed man in the squat-legged chair. His own eyes moved down past the mass of parents and children. By the stations. Jesus is scourged and crowned with thorns. Past the side altar to Our Lady. Jesus meets the women. Past the curate's confessional. Veronica wiping the face of Jesus. Picture of Jesus' face left behind on the towel like a photograph. Jesus falls the first time and the sacristan standing by the main doors. Then up again by the far wall. Jesus falls the second time. His father at the back of the church in his lonely pew, under the ninth station. Aloof from the crowd, with a uniformed guard on either side of him. One of the guards whispered something to the hunched-up man. But the boy turned back towards the bishop, towards the whispering children and towards his mother, who looked neither to left nor to right, before his father might catch him looking.

By the time his request had been processed and granted, McKenna had decided that he no longer wanted to be present at his son's confirmation. Now as he sat, a publican to the curiosity of the crowd in the main body of the church, he could understand why. His wife hidden among the ranks of suits and skirts, was sat with her back towards him. His son, he felt, was afraid to turn and look down the aisle. McKenna glanced about the church. At the bishop in his chair, at the altar boys in their pew, at the parish priest twitching nervously before the crowd. He thought of the journey up from Portlaoise that morning. Up through the flatlands of Laois and Kildare. An accident just outside Naas. An articulated truck across the road. Hoping the journey would have to be cancelled. The guard beside him

102

trying to reassure him.

—We'll make it alright. Sound as a bell.

Then the journey up by the river and the crowds on the quays and the church. And the woman refusing to give him eye and the boy stealing glances from time to time. He lowered his head once more, taking his eyes from those about him.

How long has it been? Near six years. And what about it, anyway? More cars on the road. More of a crowd in the city. Headlines there, coming in by Inchicore: Government announces new pay deal. Again. Which government? Doesn't matter a tinker's curse. See that one on the quays. Arse on her. Dear Jesus, I'd have to be dug out of you, so I would. And what did I want coming here at all for? Children and more children. And me down here on me tod. And everyone letting on I'm not here. And a guard on either side of me for company. Are you blind, woman? Wouldn't you even look back once, Maura? Wouldn't you do me that one little favour? I'm only the child's father, after all. Your husband. That's who. And he won't even do me the honour of a crooked look either. Alright, then. Curse of Jesus on the both of you!

Calm down, Jack. You're getting yourself all aeriated.

That's what you'd say now, isn't it? With the mournful face on you. And what about your new boy? A few years older than me, by all accounts. Class of a socialist, I hear. Telling other people their own business. And what do you do of an evening, the both of you? I suppose you hoosh up to the fire and gabble on about politics, do you? Look! Look! There's your wee parish priest man tripping over his feet again. That ould boy should be put out to pasture. And see him up there? Chap with the big hat. Lifting up his hands now, he is. Great ones for the bit of theatre, all the same. I can just see the two of you, your little man spouting on about all kinds of Stickie stuff and you getting your little bit in every so often. You were never stuck for the witty phrase, Maura, I'll grant you that. Like the time you said to me:

That's you, Jack. Give away your arsehole and shit

through your ribs. What use is that to anyone?

And how right you were, Maura. Soft Jack. Easy-going Jack. Jack-the-lad. And no, I don't begrudge you your bit of happiness. It wasn't easy living with me. I know that. But it was the time that was in it too, Maura. We were all gone mad then. All carried away by the whole business. If we'd won then, they'd be all writing books about us now. Flag waving and up this and down that. And the New Lodge and the thirteen and the Kesh and all. The last round. This is it. It was my bad luck to be caught driving the car that day. If I hadn't to have got jumpy at the roadblock out in Saggart, we would've been away. And it was an accident. He didn't mean to. None of us wanted that. Still, I would have had a run-in, one way or the other. I suppose you know that the appeal is likely to be turned down again, don't you? It was a long shot anyway. Look! Is that him? No, it just looked like him. The hair, you know. Good-looking, like his father. You have him well togged-out, anyway. But that's what really gets me, Maura. The thought of you there with him. With this other fellow. I don't even know his face. Jesus Christ, weren't we the fools.

You should think, Jack. Think before you act.

Roses, roses all the way. And the cute boys. They must be all smiling at us now up in Leinster House. And much good it does me being bitter about it either. Won't get me out a day earlier. There you are, Johnny boy. Caught your eye that time, didn't I, son. Not quick enough for your ould da, no matter what that up- the-workers monkey tells you. Bit on the small side you are, though. Has he set you against me, Johnny-I-hardly-knew-you? Smokes a pipe, I hear. Great man for the books. Let him. But the thought of you all together.

We're happy, Jack. That's the main thing.

That's what you'd say, Maura, isn't it? Like you said to me once. When we lived in that chalet down on the South Beach out in Rush. Bottle gas and near-pneumonia and not a penny to spare. And what will I do when I get out? England, maybe. Nothing here now. And I still love you both. So I must leave. Not look back. Not even once. And you are looking better, Johnny. Not that funny look in your eyes. Not that queerness that got into you there for a while. What was it? Did it all get to you, son? Maybe you were taking it in all the time. Small and all as you were. Me and your mother fighting. Raids at all hours of the night. Every time a cat farted. That didn't help, I suppose. And that's all it took. One shot. And here we are. What?

—We were told you could have a few extra minutes after, you know. If you want, like.

—How do you mean?

—In the school. The two of you. Unofficial, like. You needn't let on.

They watched as the bishop gave his final blessing and, followed by the four altar boys, made his way back into the sacristy. Flashes from small cameras. Children lined up along the altar rail with their parents. In the background, the sacristan moving about in silence, rearranging all without purpose. McKenna could see them both now. His wife and the boy, as they made for the side door, carried along by the momentum of the crowd. When the last of the children had left, and the church fell once more to the old women in the side aisles, they crossed through the alleyway into the school. They passed under the reams of bunting along the corridor, by paintings and motifs on the walls. A placard at the entrance to the school hall said:

We are all Gods,
children

A large man stumbled by them bearing, unsteadily, an enormous tea-urn. They were ushered in silence into the principal's office, by a younger teacher who appeared ill-at-heart in the role delegated to him.

The heating had been turned on in the hall for the morning. There were trays of pink fairy-cakes and trays of white fairy- cakes. The older children moved between the tables pouring strong tea from the catering kettles which had been borrowed for the occasion from the women's committee. A large cake sat on a stand at the top of the hall. A lone photographer, who had managed to slip in past the caretaker, went from table to table touting for custom. From time to time, one of the teachers standing by the windows would feel himself obliged to cross over to one of the family tables to make conversation. When the bishop arrived a nervous silence descended upon the room. Led by the parish priest, he stopped at each table in succession. Some insisted that he stand into a photograph with the family. Others were content with a handshake or a mumbled salute. Maura, sitting quietly with the boy, wondered when the signal would be given. She assumed that it would not be necessary to speak to her husband before the eyes of the other parents and the staff. The bishop was saying a few words now. He raised up his hands as he had done in the church. She turned her eyes away from the crowd and the tall man by the cake-stand.

—Now, boys and girls, you'll look back on this day and you'll say to yourselves, 'Well, wasn't I very young and innocent then?' Oh, the best days of your life are your school-days. And I'm sure all the mammies and daddies will agree. Isn't that so? Oh, indeed and it is.

Why did you have to come at all, Jack? Was it to get at me some way? Why couldn't you leave us alone? Haven't we been through enough? You don't mean anything to us anymore. We don't hate you. We don't want to hurt you. But, as true as I'm sitting here, Jack McKenna, you won't get a chance to ruin the child's day. What if it is all my eye anyway? Isn't it a day out for him? A bit of colour. God knows he's suffered enough over the last few years.

—I'd like you to give a big hand for all the mammies and daddies. Big clap, now. Louder! Isn't that grand!

We have the flat now, I have regular hours in the shop. Michael has his own little sideline that brings in a few shillings. It's small and it's a bit cramped. But it's our home. And the child has a new father. It's a new life, Jack. I'm sorry. I don't want to hurt you. But you ask for it sometimes. And, by the way, whose that gouger you sent 'round to have a look-in last Christmas? Just out of Portlaoise.

Thin as a rake, he was. Short back and sides. One of the great liberators too, by the look of him. Well, I gave him the door. Now, don't go ruining the day, Jack. I know you're not really that mean. The child's happy. I'm happy. And we're going to meet Michael down town later on. And we'll all go off for the day. A bit of a treat. Yes, him. Michael.

—Well, aren't you the best children in the whole of Ireland! Oh, there's no doubt about it at all! The best children in the whole country.

And we're all happy together. So, leave us be. That's all I'm asking you. Is that too much to ask, Jack?

There was a man standing at her shoulder, dressed in a dark suit and tie. He coughed politely as he spoke, glancing about him at the eyes of the hall.

—Mrs McKenna, they're waiting on you above in the principal's office. If you'd like to follow me, please.

She laid her hand on the boy's shoulder as they followed the caretaker along the cold corridor. Past bicycles chained to the staircase, under bunting and paper-chains into the office. Dogs barking in the schoolyard. A solitary gasfire burned in the room, but it scarcely sufficed to draw the chill from the air. Her husband was sitting in the principal's chair. One of the guards sat perched on the desk before him, while the other stood uneasy sentinel by the window. They both nodded to her as she entered the room. Her husband smiled. She noted now, the same cadaverous look she had seen about the stranger who had called before Christmas. The leanness in the face. McKenna stood up slowly and walked up to his wife and child. The taller of the two guards spoke from his position by the window.

—We can only give you the bare fifteen minutes. That's the way it is.

When McKenna went down on one knee to embrace his son, the woman stood back. The boy stared straight ahead, over his father's shoulders. At the serge trousers and the desk-top laden with books and the gas-heater muttering away harmlessly by the open window. His father was pressing a coin into his hand. His father was winking at him.

—You're a big lad now, Johnny. Listen to me, son, if that ould boy with the funny hat gives you a clatter won't you come and tell your da? I'll soon put manners on him, so I will.

He pressed his fist against the boy's cheek. The child countered with a wary smile, as if recounting some past incident to himself. As if he felt that, at any moment, his father might jump up and make a run for the free air. His mother's hand was on his shoulder again. He heard her whisper something to the caretaker. His father was standing now, shifting uneasily from foot to foot. Without leave to glance back at his parents, the boy was escorted out of the room by the caretaker. As they made their way back down the corridor towards the hall, they could tell, from the sound of children running about, that the bishop had already left.

The two guards stood together by the windows. One looked out onto the empty street, while the other kept an eye on the couple sitting in the far corner of the room. McKenna sat as a penitent might before a confessor. He fidgetted with the cigarette in his hand, finding it hard to keep his eyes on the woman before him. His wife understood that she must touch him, though she did not. She contented her hands with the clutch-bag on her knees.

—He's in great form, so he is. Big change there.

—They told me at the hospital that he's more or less out of it.

—That's great news. I was worried there for a while.

—All under control

—I know. I know.

They spoke of the new appeal. There was very little option now, he told her, but to resign himself to serving out the full sentence. When they drew near to discontent, the woman fell silent and looked away. He complimented her on her dress and she acknowledged his comments smartly. When she spoke of her present situation, she took care to talk in the first person at all times. She told him about the flat they had been given by the Corporation.

Three rooms, but no bath. Older flats. How she had run from one TD to the next for help, before finally receiving a sympathetic hearing from one of the new Socialist Party deputies.

—He's mixed up with them ones, isn't he?

—Who? What do you mean?

—The new man. Michael, isn't that his name?

She opened her handbag. The eyes were taunting her now. The feet shifting agitatedly. She came upon a cigarette. He offered her his own to light it from. She handed back the cigarette. She avoided the eyes even as she spoke.

—There's no point to this, Jack.

—I don't suppose there is.

—Look, I know you have your feelings. I know that.

—Poor wee Jack.

—Stop it! Now!

She drew hard on the tobacco and eyed the guards by the window. The smaller man was looking at his watch. The uniformed men whispered together. Her husband had fallen into a gloomy silence now. He seemed almost inconsolable to her. Her thoughts ran from the man before her. She thought of the boy who might be sitting alone in the hall now.

The hall had grown chill as the families gathered themselves together to leave. The older girls went about clearing up the serviettes, the paper plates and the cups. Only a few sandwiches had been touched. The principal gave orders that the left-overs be wrapped up and sent over to the convent for the charity teas later on that evening. The caretaker went about sweeping between the tables and replacing the posters which had fallen down with the heat. The boy was sitting alone at a table close to the cakestand. Nobody spoke to him. He sipped at the cold tea in the paper cup and wondered about his father and his mother. Would they be arguing now? Or just sitting in silence as they used to? A horse and cart passed by outside. Two boys were shouting to one another as they drove along. A tall, red-haired youth waved towards the teachers standing by the end of the window. One of the older men laughed.

—McGrail! Oh, a useless article if ever there was one. A right little waster.

—Like father, like son.

The boy turned to watch the woman who had spoken. The teachers were smiling to one another. They were talking about the cart boy's family. About his mother, who always had a stink of drink on her breath. About the boy's father, who hadn't worked in twenty years and wasn't in any hurry to either. The teachers said. He wondered whether they spoke of his own father and mother in that way. His father's moustache and the way he clenched his fists. His accent was harder than his mother's. It was much sharper. He would never be fat either, his mother had said. That was because his father took a lot of exercise down in Portlaoise. Not like Michael. Michael sat and read and made things with his hands. Sometimes Michael too sat in silence. But it was another sort of silence. A happier silence, that wasn't waiting for an argument to resolve it. Michael with his soft hands and his thinning hair and the belly when he wore the cords his mother didn't like. Always books around him, and people calling around to the flat in the evening to talk with Michael and his mother. They talked about the country and money and politics and laughed a lot. Michael sometimes told jokes.

The teachers were moving away from the table now, as if sensing that the boy was listening in on them. He wondered what would happen if his father, if Jack-the-lad were to visit the flat now. His father's light footsteps all the way up the staircase. And if he came and sat by the fire next to Michael. And if his mother sat in between them, just in case a row started. The coals blazing in the hearth. The china dogs on the mantelpiece. His mother would sit sipping a sherry. Michael would have a six-pack of stout at his feet. His father would not drink though. His mother intervening whenever the two men came close to quarrelling. Michael and Jack-the-lad would talk, and he and his mother would listen.

* * *

The boy lies listening on the fold-down bed in the corner. Maura tucks him in. Then she crosses over to the fire once more and resumes her place between the two men. At every sharp word she starts. Michael reaches across her for the bottle-opener. Four flights below, a bus heaves by along the busy street. Someone is arguing with a doorman outside the pub across the road.

—Are you alright there, lads?

—We're grand, Maura. Grand.

McKenna, her husband, does not answer, but nods instead in quiet confirmation. The boy stirs in his bed. The woman glances over her shoulder. McKenna straightens himself up in the easy chair as he speaks.

—Listen, Michael. Sure I can't even cross a road now without getting the shakes. And what's it worth to me now? All that time I done down there?

—I can't answer that for you, Jack, it's all past, though. Isn't that the way you have to look at it?

—That's very easy said. Very easy said. But when was the last time they came and locked you up?

—That's not the point.

—Oh, but it most certainly is the point.

—Jack …

—Maura, what I'm saying is that at least we fought for what we believed in. That's all. Nothing more.

There is quiet as they sit with their drinks, whiling away the moments in silent reflection. McKenna speaks first, as if with some secret he cannot but share.

—Them ones will never learn any other way, so they won't.

—But where does that get us?

—Isn't it better to bring it all out into the open, well? To have done with it?

The child coughs in his sleep. The woman rises to tend to him. She rouses him to take a spoonful of sweetened medicine. When he lies back again, she goes out to the kitchen and busies herself with the tidying-up. She keeps an ear to the talk in the front room.

—You lot down here know nothing about it anyway. Sweet shag all.

—Well I'm sorry to have to disagree with you. Some of us do know something. And, what's more, we think that things have gone on the same way far too long.

—Well, God love you, all the same! Haven't you had a hard time of it. Do you really believe that men — and women too — who've gone to jail for what they believe in are going to drop everything at the say-so of some Free State minister? I would have given you credit for a bit more wit, Michael, so I would.

—It won't be easy.

—Like fun it won't. From the centre to the sea, Michael. It's the only way in the long run. And what's more, you know it in your heart.

—One last push? Is that it?

—That's about the size of it.

—Are you ready for something to eat?

The woman's voice calls from the tiny kitchen. She is worried about the child now. She feels that he is fretting in his sleep. He has started coughing again. She asks the men to lower their voices. By the fire, she sets down a plate of sandwiches and a small jar of mayonnaise. McKenna, her husband, stands up to stretch himself as she adds coal to the fire.

—Grand wee flat.

—It does us for the time being.

—Warm it is.

—You'd heat it with a candle. The size of it.

—You would, right enough.

They eat the sandwiches and stare ahead of them into the open fire. Sounds about them. Children playing in the stairwell. Two women chatting together outside a door. Traffic beating by along the busy street below. Maura lights a cigarette. The others do not smoke. Her husband's eyes are on her. But she looks neither to her left, nor to her right. She keeps her gaze set on the flames before her. McKenna picks at the fire with a stout poker. He shrugs his shoulders. He waves the poker before him as he speaks.

He smiles.

—You lot had it too bloody easy down here, so you had. That's what's wrong with you.

—And would you wish all that on us so?

—What I'm saying, Michael, is that it was grand and easy to play footsie with the North when it suited you. There was nobody like us there, for a while. The poor wee North. The poor Catholics are being trampled on again. We weren't used to that, you see. So it went to our heads. We believed you. And more fool us. And now that things have got rough again, you don't want to know us at all.

—Sure we all know that.

—And you know what they say too, don't you?

—What do they say?

—Scratch any Southerner and you'll get a Free Stater underneath.

—Ah, go 'way out of that.

—The truth is seldom sweet. But yous'll get your come-uppance one of these fine days.

The doorbell rings. Maura comes out from the kitchen to answer the caller. She speaks with the woman at the door before going back into the kitchen again and returning with a small packet. The child on the couch stirs against the cold air from the open door and draws the blankets tighter. The men move in towards the fire. The woman takes her place again before the flames.

—Move in there, Maura, and get yourself a heat.

—I'm grand now, Jack.

—Well, that's my word on it anyway, Michael.

The older man smiles at him. A child is cursing another child in the stairwell. The woman laughs to herself. Michael nods his head.

—Things fall apart, the centre cannot hold; mere chaos is loosed upon the world. Have you ever heard that one, Jack?

—What are you on about? What's he talking about, Maura?

Michael stretches out and, taking up the poker, sets to ordering the fire before him.

—You know, we've all seen our share of trouble in one way or another. We can't just carry on looking for someone to blame.

—But who started it all? Would you riddle me that? Burntollet and Samuel Deveney and Bloody Sunday? Who started it all, I'm asking you?

—We could go on like this all night.

—You don't want to give me an answer, Michael, because you are afraid to. You might have to think twice about your stickie mates.

—Jack …

—Alright, Maura. I'm only saying. That's all.

—Are you ready for a cup of tea?

—Cup of tea will do rightly, Maura.

She goes off into the kitchen to scald the pot. The men sit uneasily together now. Michael takes a pipe down from the mantelpiece and scrapes out the charred tobacco of the day with a penknife. He speaks softly, looking up from time to time at the man next to him.

—You see the thing is, Jack, that I agree with you in one way.

—Do you, now?

—I do. In one way.

The woman comes into the sitting-room with a tray on which she has laid a teapot, sugar-bowl and milk-jug, three cups and a plate of plain biscuits. Michael stands up to take the tray, but continues speaking in a lowered voice.

—You see, we can't just walk away from the problem. We can't turn our back on the North. It's too dangerous.

—Is that more of your socialist cant?

—Maybe it is. I don't know. But I remember hearing somebody putting it very well there a while ago. At a meeting. He said it was like a man standing on a railway platform. A blind man.

—Two?

—One'll do, Maura. Go on with your blind man.

—And he hears a train pass, you see. And he wants to hop down onto the tracks to cross to the far side. So he says to himself: 'Grand. Train's gone. Off we go.'

—Get to the point, will you, for Christ's sake!

—Milk?

—Just a drop. That's it! Anyway, he's half-way across the tracks when doesn't he hear the sound of another train coming. Where were you then? He doesn't know what to do. Will he run back across the Northern track or carry on across the Southern track? He can't see and he can't trust his ears either.

—Aye and maybe you're all hearing things and there's no train coming at all. Listen, I hope that tea's good and strong there, Maura. I'm parched from sitting in front of this fire all evening.

—But the point is, Jack, we don't know. We can't trust our ears anymore.

—Away off with yourself, Michael! What do you be thinking about? Is that how you pass your days?

—Jack, remember what we said. Remember what we agreed on.

—Never worry, Maura. No problem. Michael's a bit confused in himself. That's all. With his trains and his blind boys.

McKenna stands to stretch himself. He glances over at the boy sleeping on the couch. The older man in the chair pokes the fire and settles back into silence. By the time the woman finishes her cup, McKenna, her husband, has already reached for his coat and cap.

* * *

The boy looked about him once more. The teachers had left the hall now and most of the clearing up had been done. Only a few children remained behind. He watched them for a while, as they ran about the chilled hall, drawing along behind them the crepe streamers which had tumbled down from the walls. He walked over to the windows to gaze out upon the progress of the street without. A wizened, leathern-faced, old woman was dragging a trolley behind her on the far side of the street. A child with a stick was chasing a dog over near the car park. He angled his head to try and take in the school side of the street. The caretaker had told him that his mother would be along shortly. He wondered whether he might not catch a last glimpse of Jack-the-lad before he left the school. His father, with the jumpy eyes and the long fingers. His father who couldn't sit still for one minute. His mother said. He looked both to his left and to his right but saw no sign of the man.

Then, all of a sudden, his mother was there, with his overcoat in her hand. For it had started to drizzle now and he must keep his suit dry until they reached the café at least. She did not mention the man she had just left, nor the gentle, loveless kiss she had tendered him on parting. Nor the bitter chanting of her heart as she sat alone in the office, counting out each footfall until she could hear no more. For there was no more to be thought about the matter. And she had dried her eyes and settled her dress. Making for the river, they passed the church and a couple arguing with a child over something they had left behind during the ceremony. And once on the quays again, they walked smartly towards the city centre, in order not to keep Michael waiting and to out-fox the heavy clouds bearing slowly up the river from the cold east.

When the Sun Bursts

HER EYES WERE TROUBLED by the glare of the screen. And the receiver spool had jammed a couple of times as well. She was about to engage the text once again, when the librarian appeared at her side.

—I'm sorry about that, but there doesn't appear to be any additional material. Just the collector's name.

—O'Neasáin of Cooley. Wasn't that what it was?

—That's the name alright. If you'd like to check through the microfiche again. Just in case.

Eilish Grace adjusted her glasses and re-read the extract. The tale, culled from the telling of an incident which had taken place more than a hundred years before, touched her deeply. She felt for the young girl whose name sat on the screen. The awful world of poverty and agrarian violence in which she had lived. Sour vengeance done to tithe-proctors. Cattle grazed by stealth at night. A poacher sent for transportation for the soul of a stewed rabbit. The tale itself was set in that region which lies under the shadow of Slieve Gullion. Perhaps the folklore collector himself was still alive? The account had been collected in 1920, when the girl who had witnessed the incident would be an old woman. The collector would have to be that old himself now, if he were still alive. And men not living that long, the woman at the screen surmised, perhaps he was not. Women were given that bit extra, she suspected, to make up for what they lost through bearing and rearing. Wasn't there some folk-tale she had come across an age ago, which explained how women had been granted longevity over men? Some Eastern tale, she suspected.

She turned the spool again and considered the name on the screen: Catherine Connaughton. A poor girl, by an ill-hour, chancing on an evil deed. Eilish Grace reminded herself that she must call up to see her son and his family sometime during the week as she had promised. The children would be in front of a screen too, with images of further realities in their eyes. They would probably speak little to her. They scarcely seemed to have time to speak with their parents even. Their childhood would be a childhood of loose images and catchphrases. It was an eon away from the circumstances of the girl whose name was before her on the microfilm reader. She looked back to the screen and read on.

—It was Willie McMorrow. Listen Catherine, says he. Take them grippers with you, says he. And go and attend your cow, like a good girl. And when I was driving the cow out of the field, I heard this commotion in the other field. In the Hen McArdle's field. So I stole a look through a gap in the shouch and I saw Willie McMorrow and these other two men and they beating this poor fellow with their sticks. And they beat him dead, so they did. I didn't know rightly what I should do, for I was near dead myself with the fright of it all.

(MS 3408 p120)

The young girl Catherine Connaughton does not move. One of the men shouts again and draws a kick at the huddled figure. She bites her lip. The cow moves on up the lane. She turns from the gap and crouching, steals along by the ditch towards the gate. She makes her way back towards the village with the beast. It stops from one moment to the next to tear at clumps of grass along the way. Behind her, the voices still. As she turns into the yard at the edge of the village, she meets with the Dolan boy. She should not tell what she has seen, but she does anyway. The cow saunters off towards the furthest corner of the yard. The Dolan boy laughs at her. She hunts the beast into the dry patch and crosses to her parents' house. Later on that same evening, in her uncle's public house down in his village, she serves the custom. At ten o'clock, Willie McMorrow and his companions arrive in. They are full and loud. McMorrow pays her no heed and her uncle serves him. All the while, she

*busies herself with the pots and will not let the raised sticks
of the afternon unsettle her memory. At about midnight,
McMorrow and his companions stumble towards the door.
McMorrow calls across to her before he leaves. She is a
grand, quiet class of a girl, he says. Not like some of the
tramps that does be around the town. A girl the like of her
would surely know the value of a silent woman. Wouldn't
she?*

Eilish Grace had spent the last couple of months hounding a theme and running her sources to earth. And now it all seemed such a vain endeavour to her, for the main focus of her enquiries, the testimony of the girl Catherine Connaughton, had run dry almost in mid-sentence. For the whole tone of the proposed paper on 'Agrarian unrest in the early nineteenth century as represented in the oral tradition', had been taken from the accounts given by Catherine Connaughton to the collector O'Neasáin. Why hadn't she checked the run of the material before committing herself to such a narrow field of enquiry? She should not have relied on a general survey of the sources. Was it age which was turning against her? Or had vanity touched her reason and led her astray? She might discuss the matter with her son, Richard, later on that week. If he was unable to counsel her, he might at least give an indulgent ear. When her sister May came up from Cork for the few days, as she always did before Easter, she might derive some solace from her good cheer. For the moment, however, she must cleave to the way she had followed over the past couple of months. She stood up wearily and switched off the screen. The grey of the mid-morning sky caught her eye through the library window. She took up her folder and handbag, smiling at the craving for coffee which had suddenly siezed her. With the indifferent authority of old age, she strolled slowly across the concourse towards the cafeteria.

In the college cafeteria, she watched the history men at the next table. Before her stood a cup of coffee. She stirred the cup idly as she watched the men. She noted with gentle disdain the furtive genuflections in the voices of the junior lecturers when their seniors spoke. They were like little dogs, she mused. All tugging at the one bit of marrowless bone. Now that she had retired from official duties herself, she felt more comfortable in the company of her colleagues. There was time for thought and talk now. The constant of preparing lectures was no more. She need give account of herself to no-one. And there were threads she chanced to take up every now and then. It might be the spur of rediscovering one of Stith-Cross's folk motifs in some older material. It might come about by way of some stray comment made by a colleague. The tale of the Connaughton girl, however, had involved her as no other had for a long time. In easy moments, Eilish Grace would reminisce to herself about the middle years of the Folklore Commission, when she herself travelled far and wide for fresh material for the archives. Old men and women smiling at her hapless diligence as they scored their stories into the scuffed face of a magnetic tape. She had often pondered the morality of her work too. Tearing talk from strangers. And the tricks she had learned in order to goad speech from her sources. A mention of a child's illness or some comment about a neighbour. There was something her late husband Matthew Grace had said to her one night too.

—Culture. As soon as you pause to look at it, you kill it. Fades in the light. Light destroys it.

And that other thing he had said when she had a paper published in a Festschrift in honour of some German scholar.

—You've probably met some of the sweetest-talking scoundrels in the country on your rounds, Eilish. Your business is to elevate their lies in academic circles.

Was Matthew Grace a jealous man, then? But she was distracted once more by the history men, who seemed to be squabbling over the fate of a government. When the head of the department spoke, all listened. She heard the well-rounded vowels, saw the resonance of his reasoning in their faces. A South Dublin accent, born of the loins of social necessity. It seemed to her to be a careful compromise between a received standard British accent and a transatlantic one. Opaque it was. An accent which might reveal a destination without hinting at a starting-point, whether rural or urban. That was its purpose, she thought. She turned her face from the history men. No! Matthew Grace had not been jealous. Just uneasy that he had been forced to bend his temper to a job he hadn't particularly wanted. Sub-editing on a morning newspaper, working into the awkward hours of the morning. Thunder of the presses. Words on newsprint sailing by a man with a monkey wrench. Click-clack of the linotype machine. A hundred thousand words arranged and rearranged each day and then discarded. Not like the oral tradition. Print was certainly the weaker of the two. And Matthew Grace's books, those he had written himself, lying unread in a hundred libraries.

—Mrs Grace?

She looked up from the table. There was a young, dark-eyed woman standing there. Could she interrupt her for a moment? The younger woman brushed her hair back over her shoulder as she spoke. It would only take a minute.

—Sit down, girl. What was it you wanted?

—It was really about the schools' survey, Mrs Grace. The 1937 collection.

—Ah, yes.

—I tried to catch you in the library earlier.

—And what was it exactly you wanted to find out?

—I'd like to discuss the work with you. On a general basis. It relates to a paper I have to write.

—Well, I could go over some of the indexed summaries with you. That sort of thing. My memory isn't too clear on the details, of course.

Eilish Grace thought back to the schools' collection and the thousands of submissions she had sifted through. Stories my grandmother told me. There was a man in our town once. My father says it's unlucky to eat eggs off of a silver spoon and my mammy says we'll never get the chance anyway. And the Child of Prague would be left out under the bushes the night before the wedding. For a bad rash, you boil dock leaves. A hunchback who could curse. My grandfather says, that when you don't hear the corncrake no more, you'll know the world is in a bad way. *The corncrake falls silent.* That sort of thing was just an inverted form of the death messenger motif, she thought. Decline of external token coincides with decline of subject. All the folkloric jargon which had grown as the body of lore actually declined. People did not tell stories anymore. They talked about stories. And the poor corncrake, like the banshee, calling out before the cataclysm. A bit like myself, Eilish Grace thought. A solitary wail. But there were other, subtler forms of the same motif, she felt. She recalled that summer, a few years previously, when she had taken a break in Zurich from work on some marginalia in St Gallen. The walks she had taken down by the Zurichsee. The sight of the sickness shocked her — the children of the rich, taken by heroin. Her hosts back in St Gallen scorned her explanation. What did she mean by saying that she had seen a sign? The answer was quite simple.

—*Zu viel Geld. Sie haben zu viel Geld, Frau Grace.*

Ah no, she thought. It's not that they have too much money at all. They suspect, these young ones, that there is no future for Europe. That the shadow in their hearts will one day unite with the greater shadow without. The shadow of a thousand suns. What was the poem by that Japanese fellow again?

—When the sun bursts again
And we are blinded again
And the shadow of a thousand blazing noons
Falls on our children and their seed.

Beasts swarming before the sun bursts. Was the last age of Europe to be consumerism then? First you consume objects, then you consume people. Frantically dulling our senses to avoid the imponderable awfulness of it all. Last dance before the sun bursts. Like those terrible damned souls she had read of who, on their way to Auschwitz, rutted with one another in the anonymity and the foetid darkness of the rail wagons. No corncrake anymore. No grandparents either. No memory, no past. Only the menacing present.

—Thank you very much for your help, Mrs Grace.

—Not at all. Tomorrow morning at ten o'clock, then?

—That's fine.

Eilish Grace watched the girl walk away, realising that she had scarcely heard a word spoken. The steady sway of the hips, the sheen of the henna highlights in her hair. She watched the girl ascend the stairs. She considered another notion she had often entertained: that generation was female. That seed and line were to be counted through the dam, not the sire. The turntailing male could be black-widowed out of the whole process without much to-do. Wasn't there a painting she had seen on the same theme somewhere? Zurich again. Yes Kunsthaus. Painting showing women giving birth to women giving birth to women. Then why wasn't the idea represented in the oral tradition? Because the traditions were dominated by men? No, too glib that. Perhaps a conspiracy between both to hide the truth. She was sure she didn't know.

The history men stood up to leave. One of them nodded to her kindly and she smiled. They passed before her with their trays as they made for the kitchen hatches. A thin, bespectacled lecturer brought up the rear. She watched with relish as he bumbled along behind the others in a vain effort to keep the conversation turning. She stood to leave and set her chair back in its place. What would a daughter of her own have looked like? How they might have grown together. It wasn't the same with grandchildren through a son. A son wouldn't turn to a mother for advice on rearing children. A daughter would. Women bearing women bearing women. She rose from the table and returned her tray to the hatch. It was sometimes possible to think far too much, Eilish Grace felt. Those with the least self-knowledge had always seemed to her to be the happiest of all. Those who felt. For thought was cheap. Far better to spend the day in idle chatter than in unsettling intro-spection. She must beware of too much thought. Under a menacing grey sky, she drove out of the college for the inner suburbs of the city.

Within half an hour, she was back in her own house in Harold's Cross. The suburb of Harold's Cross, along whose perimeter lay a canal, a hospice for the dying and a cemetery, teetered awkwardly between the civility of Rathgar and the working district of Kimmage. Its red-brick walls, almost gnawed away by a hundred damp winters, seemed constantly set to topple. It was, in some ways, a quarter of widows and the dead of an older, smaller city. And that was why Eilish Grace and her late husband had chosen to reside there. On the street in which she lived the rump of Protestant gentility still draped their doors with striped canvas to protect the paintwork from the summer sun. There was little through-traffic and there were few children. Gardens were tended and people worried about break-ins and any houses let to tenants. At home once more, she set to distracting herself with the notes she had taken earlier that day. Eilish Grace was uneasy about using her late husband's study in the return. It should not have to suffer the undue attention of broom and brush. For this reason, she had arranged all the material for the forthcoming paper in the sitting-room. There were photocopies, reference books and maps of Armagh about her on the floor. She lit the gas fire and sat back with her papers. Eilish Grace was not an appealing-looking woman, but her face showed a marked kindness of nature. She always wore flat shoes and was inclined to shuffle about the house when on her own. There was a cardigan for every day of the week and she occasionally allowed herself a cigarette in moments of high dudgeon. Although she kept the fashion of fish on Friday, she did not consider herself to be anything more than a common member of her communion. In the fading of religions, she sorrowed more for the loss of colour than for the loss of faith. She took a tint in her hair from time to time, for she believed that a woman should not allow herself be drawn under completely after the death of a spouse. Alone in the house, she would often speak to her late husband as though the walls themselves were the repository of his spirit. She considered this to be neither obscene nor deviant. Sometimes she laughed, in the company of Matthew Grace's spirit, over the days long gone. That night, though, she slept an uncertain sleep. Did she meet with her bridegroom in her dreams? She was not sure. Perhaps he had whispered a caution in her ear.

—Vanity! Go back, Eilish! Go back!

She remembered waking in the early morning and sensing with a terrible certainty, that chilling camaraderie which life and death seem to forge at such an hour. Was sleep a crossroads between the two planes? Who was to know? She forbade herself to think anymore on the matter. That her faith failed to help her brace her nerves before the thought of death, she accepted. It was a trying and unfathomable disappointment to her. After a whispered prayer and a furtive glance at the cross above her head, however, she fell to an easy sleep once more.

ASH WEDNESDAY

She returned to the college. She had made her decision — should she find no satisfaction in her fresh search, she must turn the theme of her paper into another headwind, despite her misgivings. In the afternoon, on the spur of a chance notion, she happened upon the English version of the collector Ó'Neasáin's name among a file of miscellaneous folklore material. And there, in the distinctive autograph of John Neason of Cooley, lay additional material from the oral evidence of Catherine Connaughton. Eilish Grace scolded herself for not having considered the possibility earlier. She drew the microfilm across the track. There was an account of snaring rabbits and the tale of a priest's daughter. There were remedies for the relief of gout, of wind and croup. There was a story of a blind woman who could tell tomorrow. And there, in among the medley of anecdotes were the words of Catherine Connaughton.

—And they came to our door, so they did. And they had a warrant for to take me to jail. For I wasn't safe anymore with the Ribbonmen about. The Ribbon had their signs, do

125

you see. And the chastisers knew one another by the signs. I don't rightly know how it went now. But it might be the way they would nod at one another or maybe a wee sort of a sign they would make with their fingers. My father, God be good to him, knew all about this. And says he to the men, says he: 'Take the girseach now, for we can't look out for her ourselves at the minute.' And I was howling and I kicked the table and my father says: 'If you'd not been so free with your tongue, girl, there'd be no call for this at all. And won't you be back with us again in a wee while?' And may God forgive me, didn't I call my own father a liar. To his face. For I'd heard an uncle of mine saying that they'd maybe have to send me off to America. The way there'd be no vengeance taken on me. And, Mister Neason, I spent the best part of a year in Armagh Jail, so I did. And there was every kind of streel and tramp in it. Women you wouldn't meet with in the Black Hole of Calcutta. And some of them had their babies with them, you know. Oh, yes. Wee scrawny bits of things they were too. Well, I was sick in it and I was sad in it. And there was a minister and a priest come by every Sunday to say their services. And they would pass one another on the long corridor and they wouldn't as much as nod to one another, so they wouldn't. And I was the youngest in it. Bar a certain street-girl, the name of Agnes. And me and Agnes would sit near to one another when we'd get our food and we'd talk about our homes. But she had no father, as far as she could make out anyway, this Agnes girl. And sometimes we'd cry together and say we'd as soon be dead, God forgive me, as where we were. And a year, Mister Neason, a whole year I spent in Armagh Jail until the trial came about.

Catherine Connaughton sits out her first night in the prison and does not sleep. The women in the cell do not trouble her with talk. She hears shouts about her. A mad-woman is screaming something about a warder. Then, a cell door is kicked. Catherine Connaughton draws a blanket about her. When the first light comes, she falls to sleep. She is awoken a short time later by the unbolting of the doors. The women file out onto the long corridor. At table,

*she notes a girl almost as young as herself. She smiles at
the other girl. The girl turns away. Catherine Connaughton
wonders why she was chosen to witness the murder of
Deveney in the Hen McArdle's field. She is angry with the
Dolan boy for telling the tale to everyone. If the Dolan boy
had only held his mouth. If she herself had not spoken. But
the Dolan boy likes to talk and that is why she is in among
the women now. And not in Tochar Brid in her father's
house. Or driving the brindle cow up the laneway. A sweet
woman, with a pustular sore on her cheek, lays her hand
upon Catherine Connaughton's hand.*

—Get that into ye, daughter. Them ones aren't too free
with th'oul grub at all. They be's always on the lookout to
scavenge. You must take what your gev' and be grateful.
For they'll not ask you twice. Oh, they'll not ask you twice,
so they won't.

By the time Eilish Grace left the library, it was almost
five o'clock. She would have time to visit her son and his
family. She left the Arts' building by the rear doors. The
coldness of the new college campus was something to
which she had never grown accustomed. There was a feeling of dislocation about the place as though it had been
rejected by the city on whose southern flanks it squatted.
It certainly appeared to have little immediate reference to
the world about it. Why had she agreed to read the paper
at the forthcoming seminar at all? She buttoned her coat,
pausing a moment to draw her keys from her handbag.
Weren't there others who could undertake such a task far
better than she? It was vanity which had driven her to
accept the challenge. That was it. The desire to stand in
front of a forum of her juniors and hold forth. Would they
pity her, a retired lecturer from the folklore department,
with her faltering voice and the new-found innocence of old
age in her bearing? She waved across the tarmac stretch
to a visiting lecturer in the Italian department. His skin,
jaundiced by a Levantine sun, seemed quite sickly under
the low cloud cover of an Irish sky. She glanced at herself
in the driving-mirror. The dry skin, the eyes unsure of
themselves. The ashes of repentance on her forehead

which she had received at early mass in Mount Argus that morning. As she drove out through the estates at the foot of the Dublin mountains, she tried to ignore the anger constricting her thoughts. She was annoyed at herself now, for having accepted the invitation to participate in the seminar in the first place. And she was just as angry at the unknown girl called Catherine Connaughton whose voice had suddenly fallen silent in the accounts once more.

The car moved into the estate. A sign said:

WINSTON DOWNS — PLEASE DRIVE CAREFULLY

She turned into the driveway of the house. Her son had not arrived home from the city yet. The children and their mother were there. She spoke with her daughter-in-law. She sat in an easychair, watching the children watching the golden images on the screen.

—You didn't get the ashes so?

—No, we didn't.

She drank coffee, but suffered no sugar to buffer its Lenten bitterness. She spoke with her daughter-in-law. Their words were punctuated by the laughter emanating from the receiver. Eilish Grace marvelled at the way her son's wife referred to the images. The younger woman spoke of them as of the inhabitants of some small town, who were as familiar to her as she was to them. From time to time, one of the children would cast about to silence them for breaking the flow of laughter. Eilish Grace decided that she would prefer to be asleep. She turned to her daughter.

—And who has moved in next door?

—Don't know really. The husband drives a Range Rover. He's in insurance, someone said. You wouldn't know. Mark, what's the new boy's name?

—Barry. Something Barry.

—That's a Cork name. Isn't it?

—Is it? I don't know where it's from.

When it was bed-time, her daughter-in-law excused herself to put the children down for the night. The sameness of the experience in a thousand other consumer units appalled Eilish Grace. She watched the children mount the stairs. There was a folk-motif like that somewhere: *child buried alive with mother*. A sameness of age, of class, of experience. A nameless monoculture. She had no time at all for the new estates which besieged the city. She recalled something she had read by some Italian writer once, 'The new fascism,' he had called it. Object worship, a sophisticated twentieth-century animism. She scouted out the words from memory.

—I see their faces. They are nothing. They know no past. They have inherited nothing of their fathers. Their tomorrow is much the same.

She wondered whether she might work the idea into the seminar paper. But that wouldn't be allowed. She might allude to her thoughts on the matter however, far away from the printed record. Ash Wednesday to Holy Thursday. Forty days in the desert. She would surely work up something for the seminar, one way or the other. She must stop worrying. By the time her son arrived back from the city, it was nearly the hour for her to leave. She spoke briefly with the pale-faced accountant, but chose not to mention the matter of the seminar at the Academy at all. In one way, she was secretly ashamed that she had felt the urge to confide in her son. For, in truth, they had little to say to one another. Richard Grace said that he would drop over some night the following week. He smiled at her over his gold-rimmed glasses and winked at her as a token of good faith. She felt an idiot.

Over the following weeks, she concerned herself with comparing those disturbances which were reflected most clearly in both the oral accounts and the parliamentary reports. The stories of tenant agitation and of reprisals made sad reading. Whole days passed in this way. Lent and its sorry reflex in the penitential skies of spring, wore on slowly. It became obvious to Eilish Grace with the days, that she was persisting in a vain attempt to build a lecture about a fragmented and inconclusive narrative. Yet, she could not bring herself to abandon the story of the young girl from Tocher Brid. With unblinking purpose, she consistently deferred that day on which she must surely square up to the futility of her quest. What could she do? Falsify the oral account and add her own coda to the tale? It shocked her to realise that the thought had even presented itself to her. There were researchers and academics who spent their lives manipulating evidence in such a way. Packing the gallery to suit the trend of a thesis or a paper. Eilish Grace tried to keep away from herself in the evenings as much as possible. She would visit a certain neighbour for a game of whist or take a bus down to Sandymount to the bridge club. For the conflict between chance and calculation in card games had always been a comfort to her. Sometimes, as the day drew to a close, memories of a rural childhood by the banks of the Nore would come tugging at her thoughts. There were those in the village who kept the black fast throughout, as a Muslim might keep Ramadan. And there were sermons on mortification of the flesh and purification of the soul throughout Lent too. Laver of water is baptism; laver of tears is penance. The good things tucked away by her mother until Easter Sunday. Early mass and the walk past the cemetery and the creamery to the village. And you could almost tell the summer to expect, by the end of Lent. Season and sacrament beating out the time in a child's mind. The sombre colours of penance as the sky cleared and spring was borne in. But there was no use in wallowing in the past, was there?

Her sister wrote.

I will take a taxi from Kingsbridge. You may cancel your cards for the evening, Eilish. Give my love to all. Take care. See you soon.

Love,

May

ST DAVID'S DAY

The doorbell rang and she opened the door eagerly. They had not met in an age, it seemed. The two sisters embraced. May Corrigan was taller than her sister and

130

firmer of purpose. Her ginger hair was cut closer to the scalp and she always carried a clutch handbag. Wily in conversation, when she had succeeded in leading an opponent, without their knowledge, to accepting one of her own conclusions, she would say: There, now!

She had spent her working life as a matron in a Cork hospital and retired just before a newer hospital opened in the suburbs. Her late husband had been an army man. She now ran the only guest house on the Great Western Road which still refused to take unmarried couples. The walls of her house were heavy with embossed wallpapers. There were cabinets full of china dolls and brass ornaments. A sign hanging over her doorway said:

ALTEZONA

May Corrigan, on her occasional visits to Dublin, was consistently amused by the decay evident in the face of the sister city. She was not inclined to silence and had the disturbing habit of provoking arguments in company by stating the obvious. In public, as an act of defiance, she always wore a brightly-coloured scarf thrown jauntily over her left shoulder. The two widow-women talked into the early hours over a bottle of port. In the background a machine read, from a thin strip of plastic, the glowing voice of Luciano Pavarotti.

Her sister, May, would stay for a few days. There were some bits and pieces which had to be fixed up with a solicitor on the quays. They laughed together of the days of their youth. A jape played on a summer's evening long ago, by the banks of the Nore. And how they had to walk back over the fields from a dance. The curses of their father that night! Now that her sister was staying until the following week, Eilish Grace would leave the matter of the paper aside for a rest. Before she showed her sister to her room, she brought her into the study. The typewriter lay under its dustcover. There were files of newspaper clippings and shelves weary with the weight of books. There, on a shelf between Victor Hugo and *The Devil and Daniel Webster*, lay Matthew Grace's work — two short novels of South

Kilkenny and the thirties. They leafed through the books together. May Corrigan's fingers came upon an account they had often mentioned in the family. It was the story of a clash between tenants and policemen at Carrickshock during the tithe-wars of the last century. Where had he got that from actually? May Corrigan angled her head with her question.

—Would you believe this ... from a nephew of a man who witnessed the whole blessed thing. He must have been a tenant himself, sure.

Chain of transmission. One tongue, two tongue, three tongue. Real people telling of real people. When Eilish Grace lay in bed, her thoughts turned to her man. Matthew Grace, diffident and ulcerous. There were friends he had worked with from the *Independent*, she recalled. Carson, a typesetter from Phibsboro, a weasel-faced man who worried. And another one called Sullivan, a proofreader with a tendency towards whiskey, who lived somewhere off the South Circular. The frustration of her husband's life in being bound to a typewriter in a newspaper office. There were occasional displays of intemperance, which Eilish Grace bore with quiet indifference. She thought of how the man had run to bitterness near the end, with his son gone and little of his own work between his hands. There were occasional flashes of life, but the hurt of a sensitivity scorned was all too apparent in his eyes. Her heart swimming in port, her eyes troubled with tears, Eilish Grace forgave her husband once again for any ill-temper he had shown her in his life. And if they had met and never left for the city. What then? Grandchildren around them, knowing their grandparents. Where tales came by turn of mouth, not by book or screen. She told herself that she must look in the library again to see if she might unearth anything more of the story of Catherine Connaughton. She was beginning to feel a curious, illogical sense of responsibility towards the girl. She put the idea to one side. She would have a great week with May. They would have great laughs for a few days. They would go to a show together. Two right merry widows they would make! Franz Lehahr.

How does that tune go again? Oh, the way my Matthew used to dance. The feet he had and the lightness of his step. The smaller arena. To dance and to sing. I am old and a little drunk, of course. And were we happier then, in the smaller arena? With nobody looking over our shoulder? She hoped her sister did not hear her sobbing through the walls.

They went everywhere together. To the museum, to the Botanic Gardens and up to Howth Head. It seemed as if they had spent the five days in conversation. They spent a whole morning rambling about the city, touching that which was left of the past. In the snug of a pub in Chatham Street, they sipped an afternoon brandy and enjoyed a disagreement with the barman. May Corrigan turned to her sister, cocking her fringed hat in the direction of the hatch.

—Everything is supposed to be nice, do you see. Oh, they don't like it a bit when you complain. It's not nice.

In the evenings, they sat in and amused one another with reminiscences. Eilish Grace told her sister of the paper she had agreed to read at the Academy on Dawson Street. The seminar would deal with the oral tradition and recent research. She told of the young girl whose narrative would form the basis of the talk on agrarian violence. They agreed that the topic was an awkward one. There would probably be little enthusiasm for it among her audience. She must have the bones of the thing ready by the end of the month. That was clear. It had been so long since she had ventured before a crowd. May Corrigan rested her hand on her sister's knee.

—Aren't you just telling a story, sure? Isn't that all there is to it really?

—I suppose.

—And you must have a happy ending, Eilish.

—I haven't been able to find any kind of ending. That's the problem.

—Sure, can't you make it up as you go along?

—May!

In their laughter, they almost upset the vase of daffodils on the coffee-table.

On the Sunday, they walked to Mount Jerome to visit the grave. May Corrigan marvelled at the Sunday crowds thronging the cemetery. They bought flowers from a barrow and lay them by the headstone. There was a comfortable clutter to the older sections of the grounds. The bare-boughed trees stood stark against the pallor of the spring sky. Eilish Grace stood at the foot of her man's resting place, speaking with him silently. As though their conversation had suffered but the slightest interruption and the man had merely passed into an adjoining room of the same house. You hear me, Matthew, and I hear you too. I will hardly be long now, I suppose. Sometimes I am dragged down by all of this, although I know I should not let myself. I am stronger, and stronger than you ever were. For the strong, it is a sin to be weak. You are always with me. You have simply gone on ahead. That is all. But I will have my say before I go, Matthew. They will hear me out.

On the Sunday night, she saw her sister to the station. Richard had not had time to visit after all. His voice on the 'phone was without overt interest.

—Well, at least you've had a chance to communicate.

Her sister's giggled when she related what her son had told her on the 'phone. How May Corrigan threw up her arms in laughter.

—Communicate! That's what they do these days. Nobody talks to one another anymore, Eilish. Haven't you noticed that? They communicate instead. A kick up the arse is what that son of yours wants badly. With his communicate!

When her sister departed, Eilish Grace was left alone in the house by the canal, with the worry of the forthcoming seminar nagging at her once more. In her thoughts, she turned to the man who was gone for consolation. His heavy tread upon the stairs. Comrades from the paper who dropped by now and then. Friends from home who might pass a few days with them in the city. That quiet ambition he had held, to return to his own writing on retirement. How was it exactly she had been told of his death? A young man from the sports desk, she thought. That was another

folk-motif, of course: *the Death Messenger*. Eilish Grace let
her thoughts run back to the day of Matthew Grace's
death: a man without a name stands before the glass-
panelled door. Eilish Grace sees the shadow on the
coloured glass and knows unease. She is not expecting
anyone. A sense of premonition steels her tongue when she
opens the door.

—Yes?

—Mrs Grace?

—Yes?

—My name's Dermody. Tom Dermody. I work with your
husband. I wonder could I come in a minute? Matt took
some sort of a turn at work this morning.

In the study, she replaced the books they had taken
down over the weekend. She was glad she had remembered
to give her sister another copy of her husband's first book,
The Harp Has Sounded. She sat down at the davenport
and brushed the dust from the face of the desk. Another
world that was, she told herself. Not this one. The equa-
tion between time and money less certain. Children too,
more of them. Other days in *The Harp Has Sounded*, of
course. An innocent joke shared. Pleasure out of lesser
things. A world not frenzied by change. Much the same as
the world of Catherine Connaughton a hundred years
before. From the sitting-room below, the golden tones of
the tenor mobbed her thoughts. She sipped her port slowly.
And poor Catherine Connaughton, dead all those years.
Did she leave any children after her? She must really look
further afield to see if she could take up the tale again. Sitting back in the armchair, she thought of the area of South
Armagh where Catherine Connaughton had lived. The
Carrickmacross side of Crossmaglen. She had last been up
around there sometime near the beginning of the troubles.
Eilish Grace smiled to herself at an image she waylaid of
the young girl, Catherine Connaughton, casting anxious
glances over the counter of her uncle's public house at the
men drinking in the corner. She thought back to the
account in her husband's work of the murders in South
Kilkenny which would have been almost contemporaneous

with the murder witnessed by Catherine Connaughton. Of how the names of some of the dead tenants had been concealed, it was said, to avert reprisals on their families. And when Matthew Grace died himself, wasn't it practically the same thing? Hide your grief, they almost said. Never let on! Life must go on, you see. And send for a doctor in six months and turn to librium when you could no longer bear the burden of your own sadness. Dampening nature's distress with their potions. But, I knew better. And I cried, not minding what they said. And I wore widow's weeds for a full six months too. I bore my grief like a banner. If I did not hide my love, why should I hide my hurt?

There is no such thing as death now of course, she thought as she rose from the desk. Just the termination of a business arrangement. That funny phrase that someone used once. Play on who? Buber. Sort of Jewish Kung. Chap in the German department said it.

—I, Thou and you the consumer.

That was funny. But she must hunt out more material for the paper next week, one way or the other. Closing the door of her husband's study in the return, she descended the stairs once more to bolt the door for the night.

It was in the company of her child's child a few days later that Eilish Grace was struck by a possibility she had not considered before. They were in the park in Merrion Square. Watching her grandson on the climbing frame, she mouthed senseless cautions as she pondered the issue.

—Don't go up so high, Matthew. There's a good lad.

Perhaps the collector O'Neasáin had been involved in the 1937 collection? A local teacher he had been. That much was clear from the manuscripts she had seen. It would follow then, that a man like O'Neasáin would have involved himself in the schools' collection. She could not recall having seen such a name in that context though. But then, there had been so many submissions. The child jumped down onto the tarmac and raised up his arms. She lifted him up. They left the park as the last of the office workers returned to their posts. They walked in the direction of the river. Along Westland Row, woman and child stood to admire a black-and-amber train drawing itself sluggishly into the station above their heads.

—That's the Kilkenny colours, Matthew. They're the colours of the county your granny comes from.

The child smiled, innocent of her intent. On Townsend Street, she thought once more of the collector O'Neasáin of Cooley. If he were still alive, he would be an old, old man by now. She envisaged a meeting. She, Eilish Grace, sitting before an elderly man burdened by blindness and a faltering voice. The man casts back to a tale told him some sixty years before, by an old woman remembering a murder committed on a summer's day, Catherine Connaughton and the raised sticks of Tochar Brid. She must really try once more to cap the tale, even though she had failed to find any conclusion in any of the material she had unearthed in the archives. For every tale, with its chain of transmission, must have an ending. Like something she had read about the records of the oral traditions in Islam, where the line of tradition was considered almost as important as the narrative itself.

—Eilish Grace got it from Seán O'Neasáin who got it from Catherine Connaughton.

Or like that finicky habit Matthew Grace used to have, when someone interrupted him at the piano. He would always take up the tune he had been playing and tag on its tail before leaving the keys. It was unlucky not to finish a tune. You could call it petulance or superstition or asinine awkwardness. Or perhaps it was simple faithfulness to the melodic narrative in one's keeping. They crossed O'Connell Bridge and turned down Abbey Street for Marlborough Street. They bought two ice-cream cones. When they reached the Department of Education buildings, they were asked to wait in the great lobby. A man, in the orthodox dress of a civil servant of an earlier generation, questioned her. They stood together under a bust of some long-dead figure from early days of the education boards.

—And might I ask, what the precise nature of your connection with Mister O'Neasáin is?

She wiped the child's jacket. Ice-cream at this time of the year! She should really have more sense. Eilish Grace! The civil servant returned within a few minutes.

—Well, it appears that Mister O'Neasáin died quite some time ago. I have the information from pensions. I could give you the name of the last school he taught in. Would that help?

—It would, indeed.

Taking the boy by the hand, she walked out contentedly into the afternoon. A light shower of rain had fallen while they were inside and the streets glistened in a perspiration of oil and water. Little Matthew Grace was hungry again. Boys were always hungry. In a coffee shop on the corner of the street, they ate a light snack. She decided there and then that she would make one last attempt to seal the narrative of Catherine Connaughton. She would pay a visit to that quarter where O'Neasáin had spent his last days. You never knew what you might stumble on in a small village. As she scooped out the filling of a custard slice for the child, she strove hard to hide her own thoughts from herself. She could not bring herself to admit that the subject of her talk was now becoming almost secondary to the whole venture. She did not care to acknowledge that the voice of Catherine Connaughton along the line of transmission, was slowly assuming the tone of a woman in her sixty-seventh year. Of a woman who was tired of the world and ill-at-ease with the changes she had suddenly noticed on raising her head from her books. In the Pro-Cathedral, she lit a candle for her husband and for the repose of the souls. There was only a small scattering to share the silence with them. Older women like herself, for the most part. A priest, lifting aside a curtain of his confessional, knew that he had heard his last penitential narrative for the day. Stepping out into the aisle, he genuflected before the host and made for the sacristy. Into the heart of Eilish Grace, a song wound its way along a path beaten out by the simple reflexes of a melody recalled and the fragrance of incense languishing on the air.

—Virgin most pure

Star of the sea
Pray for the wanderer
Pray for me.

It was an evening in summer again. And she was a child of ten. And there was a mother and a father and a home which was sanctuary. And there were neighbours with names as well as faces. But there was no home now. Anywhere.

When she left the child Matthew back with his parents later on that evening, she thought that she had caught a glimpse of a certain duty which was hers alone. There was a duty to tell of how things had been before the advent of the nothingness. She must not break the chain. Stories were for the telling. She must not stem the source. When she lay down for sleep that night, she felt under an even greater burden than before to tell the tale of Catherine Connaughton and of the world which had ceased to be.

FEAST OF THE ANNUNCIATION

In the last week of March, with the mist upon the Mournes, Eilish Grace drove north. She struck for the area around Omeath. The last mention of the collector O'Neasáin in the files of the Department of Education concerned a small school on the shores of Carlingford Lough. It had been a long time since she had gone this road and she wondered at the wisdom of the venture. The previous evening over dinner, a friend had assured her that the journey would have its own virtue, regardless of its end. In a small schoolhouse off the main road, she made her enquiries. An elderly man, a 'walking principal', hushed the children's voices behind him. Fingers to his lips, eyebrows taut. The silence of country schoolchildren.

—Neason now. Well, he would have taught their parents. He was old when I first arrived here, of course. They say he retired to Blackrock. Just outside Dundalk. Callaghan ...

—Yes, Mister O'Dea?

—Callaghan, is your mother at home today?

—She is, Mister O'Dea. With my granny.

—That's where you'll ask, then. Callaghans. Down by the garage. Her family had some sort of dealings with Jack Neason over the years, do you see. Never married, you know. Oh, they would surely know, if anyone does.

A house by the crossroads. An old woman dandling a child. A younger woman making tea. Women strangers, at ease with one another. Eilish Grace sat drinking tea with the two women in front of the range.

—Ah, now, poor Mister Neason's dead this good ten year.

—Oh, I would say longer, Mother.

—Maybe. Well, anyway. After he gave up the school-mastering we didn't see him much at all, you know. As if he'd never set foot in the place.

—Never married.

—Home was left to a niece of his who used to look after him. Wasn't that the way of it, Kate?

—That's right. He used to drop into my mother here for the hot dinner, do you see. In the evenings, after school. Very quiet man. Oh sure, only my mother fed him, he wouldn't have survived at all.

—Kate ... Kate ...

—Yes, Mother?

A clock on the wall struck noon and the baby stirred in her sleep. The younger woman crossed to the range to settle the lid on a pot of potatoes.

—Do you mind the time someone asked Mister Neason ... ould McCormack, was it?

—What was that?

—Ah, you know well what it is I'm on about. The time McCormack the garda says to him ... says he ...'Mister Neason ... and tell me this ... confidentially like ... why is it you never have anyone 'round to your house for a drop of tea?' Well, I had to laugh, Kate! Poor ould Neason says, says he, I don't think I have enough cups. Sure, he was gone into a half idiot with them books. That's what I think personally, anyway.

—Lived for the books, Mrs Grace. And that's all fine and well, but what good is that to the world if you leave neither chick nor child after you? Now, I'll not say a word against him, so I won't. But it must have been fierce lonely for him up in that house, all on his own.

Eilish Grace considered once more, as she sipped at her tea, her sojourn in Zurich. Europe and the loss of children's voices. And the old with their pampered dogs for comfort. Was it possible, then, to consider life, from beginning to end, as no more than a series of consumer acts? As a random series of exchanges and barters and no more? She tried to visualise the man she had never met. She formed an image in her mind of Seán O'Neasáin of Cooley from the accounts she had been given by the women at the table. Tall and thin, he would be. With a turnip watch in his waistcoat pocket. Teeth stained with woodbine, eyes weak from print and page, he would constantly gaze over his pupils' heads towards something of which they were altogether too young to be aware. He would have the habit of speaking to the class without turning from the equations he was writing on the blackboard.

—A certain young gentleman is making far too much noise for my liking, Thomas Conroy.

Mind teeming with a thousand traditions he had gleaned from those around him. What a world he must have hewn from the wisdom and folly of his elders. An esoteric world to which he alone had complete access. The sort of brightly-coloured playground into which, it was claimed, a certain type of academic might regress when it became clear that the riddles of everyday life were far too arcane for comprehension.

—You could maybe drive down to Blackrock and try and hunt out the niece. She shouldn't be hard to track down.

—Aye, poor ould Neason. Sure, he was harmless too. Like a little child he was. They do say that about schoolmasters, you know. Did you ever hear that, Mrs Grace?

—What's that, now?

—They do say, and I've as often said it to Kate here myself, that schoolmasters gets like the children they teach if they stay at it long enough. Turns them quare. No job for a man, of course. Better out digging a ditch. Men don't have the wit for it. Not enough commonsense. And commonsense can't be got out of a big book neither.

Eilish Grace finished her tea and drew away gently from the conversation. When she left the women in the house by the crossroads, she decided that she would hunt no further. She drove back by South Armagh, but did not halt along the way. Not even when she passed close to that townland which she knew to be called Tochar Brid.

By early evening, she was back in Dublin again. In the house in Harold's Cross, she sifted through her notes for the forthcoming seminar. She had come to a decision. She would lay the memory of Catherine Connaughton which had so touched her these past few months. There were a couple of weeks left in which to round off the tale. She would heed May Corrigan's petulant advice and take it upon herself to cap the tale. For what was a story, anyway? Just a subjective reflex of one sort or another. And who was to say that the story of Catherine Connaughton as presented in the writings of Seán O'Neasáin was not a fiction devised for the collector's entertainment and for the distraction of academics like herself? That was it, then! She would approach the seminar on Holy Thursday with a fight in her eye. She would tell lies on her own behalf and on behalf of a girl long dead. And she would not be afraid of the men before her. And she would tell them too what she thought of the new global village. She would have her own say and tell them what she thought of this deserted village and play the corncrake with its crex! crex! crex! And if they laughed at her and hated her for it, she wouldn't care. Before sleep, she wrote to her sister and phoned her son. In sleep, she met Matthew Grace but was unsure the next morning of whether the visitation augured ill or well.

The following weeks passed quickly. Holy week was upon her before she knew it almost. She took her granddaughter for the weekend of Passion Sunday and spoiled the child with sweets and surprises. It was heartening to hear a child's voice about the house again. Once more Eilish Grace realised with shame, that she scarcely knew her granddaughter. She must really give her grandchildren more time now. As soon as the business in the Academy was over, things would change. She had spent long enough among books and the bloodless. On the eve of the seminar, she wrote in a dying language across the face of the folder in which she had arranged her lecture notes, the following words: Truth is bitter

HOLY THURSDAY

On the morning of Holy Thursday, Eilish Grace took communion at early mass in Whitefriar Street. From there, she walked past Surgeons' and down Grafton Street to breakfast in Bewleys. She kept close to her the leathern music-bag, in which she had secreted her notes. For the presence of so many people breakfasting together on a weekday had always seemed suspect to her. The idle among their number must surely have nefarious intentions upon the day. Two young women sat down before her with an unkempt child. In their pinched faces she read the inheritance of the city's poor. Eilish Grace watched the mother eat a hot-cross bun. The women smiled across the table at her. She followed their talk for a moment, before losing herself to her own speculations again. Her mind flitted from an image of her own man, to the cold, empty house near the canal, to her son who never called. It settled, finally, on a vision of the girl Catherine Connaughton driving a cow ahead of her up a laneway. A voice across the table cut in on her thoughts.

—You can't feed him in here, Cathy.

The women caught her glance. The mother of the child blushed. The under-nourished nourishing the under-nourished. Eilish Grace offered her chair to the mother as she stood up. It would be more private, being in the corner, she told them. She suspected that the mother had neither the confidence of class nor age to take the child to her breast in the crowd. The women turned away from her again, thanking her. She gathered up her gloves and the music-bag. She could hear the women talking about moving to a new flat. She nodded to them. The child smiled at her. She overheard one woman counselling the other as she took her leave.

—Either I wouldn't move, if it was me it was.

Her mind was temporarily distracted with the idea of place again until she reached the door of the Royal Irish Academy in Dawson Street. She had arrived in good time. In the vestibule, her coat was taken by a plump, cheerful woman. She passed the readers in the reading-room and paused at the entrance to the seminar room to affix a tag to her label. When she had trouble with the safety-pin, she declined assistance and threw the tag into a wastepaper basket. They would all know her anyway, wouldn't they? There would be very few women, if any. She would stand out. A junior lecturer in the archaeology department nodded to her as she entered and she took a seat near the door. A younger man leaned over a chair to shake hands with her. They heard so little of her now. She must have gone to earth altogether since her retirement. An elderly priest next to her, one of a pair, spoke to her in brittle, calloused Irish. She left her hat and gloves down on the seat beside her. The small audience did not convey the impression of great enthusiasm for the colloquium, she ventured quietly to herself. The doors behind her were closed. After the opening address had been given, a tall man with a gentle voice took the lectern. He spoke on the value of honour in the oral tradition. There were references to the Fiannaíocht and a gesture in the direction of the literature of modern Spain. Were there any general inferences which might be drawn from a comparative study of both traditions? One could be too premature, the speaker asserted in conclusion. The subsequent paper recalled the fashionable assumption of a few years previously, that certain definable links had existed between Ireland and the Mediterranean lands. The speaker declared himself opposed to the thesis. There was little evidence to be found in the oral traditions and even less linguistic evidence. He leaned forward towards his audience, in intimation of a confidence not to be recorded in the proceedings of the day.

—Or are we really, as some would haveeus believe, merely a *meitheal* of misguided Muslims facing in the wrong direction?

There was laughter and, on the lull of the applause, they broke for coffee. Eilish Grace was introduced to the few participants she did not already know. The elderly priest seemed to dog her progress wherever she went. She considered the enmities abroad in the room. Bad blood between book brothers. The haggling there might be over some academic truffle gouged out of the earth by a rival scholar. She smiled at the thought that it would all pass. Someone from Maynooth told her that he was looking forward to her lecture. Was this new research? Wasn't she a great woman, all the same. And at her age.

In the seminar room, Eilish Grace took her position at the lectern. Opening out her notes, she looked out upon the gathering. There was a solitary woman sitting in the back row, whom she had not noticed earlier. How had she missed her? She recognised neither the face nor the red hair. From some other department? Perhaps. A chance visitor? Hardly. She would address her lecture to the strange girl. That would be a good psychological ploy. The others might listen in. Or they might not. As they would choose. When Eilish Grace began to speak, she was cowed momentarily by the frail timbre of her voice. She perceived her voice, in that moment, to be no more than the crudest instrument of her intellect. She heard herself cut through the silence of those seated before her. She looked down over her reading glasses at the faces.

—And contemporary accounts from that period leave us in no doubt as to the hardship endured by both tenants and small landowners. A line graph would show quite typically, I think, a direct correlation between agrarian violence and deprivation caused by social or political forces. That this sort of agitation does not exist in a vacuum is clear from studies of contemporary similar situations in similar peasant societies. Nature cannot stand aloof from the socio-economic situation and, in the accounts to which I will refer, we shall see what some might believe to be — though not all — a fairly understandable response to what might be described as an unjust situation. I propose, in my talk, to look at one contemporary account in detail, and one which seems to fit into the pattern of agrarian violence current at the time. I hope to relate this to the general situation pertaining in the early nineteenth century. My main source will be the folklore collector Seán O'Neasáin, variously of Cooley and Omeath.

There was a shuffling of feet among the listeners and someone coughed. Eilish Grace paused a moment, then glanced at the woman sitting on her own at the far end of the room. At her red hair and her sombre dress. They smiled at one another. They won't like my lecture, of course. Muddy boots on the floor of the Academy. Sanitise all, even rural politics. Keep it cold and clear. Remove us from all sense of accountability. How would they take it, I wonder, if I told them about my little theory of folklore for the nuclear age? They might say: that poor woman hasn't been the same since her husband died. Internalisation of grieving. Some transatlantic term or other to neutralise my sorrow and make it more palatable. Yes, folklore for a nuclear age. And which motif shall we use, gentlemen? *The Death Messenger? The Fetch? Child buried alive with woman?* Oh, come on now, Father Morton! Fighting shy of the question, are we? There! You have it in one, Professor Eames! Right in one! Folk-motif for a dying world: *the Grateful Dead.* After the sun bursts, the corpses rise up, take one look at the survivors and, deciding that they are better dead, return to their rest again. Come on, Eilish! They're starting to cough again.

—We are given a graphic account of the girl's imprisonment in Armagh Jail and the rigours of life there. O'Neasáin doesn't seem to have been too upset about taking down all sorts of unpleasant details about the situation of women.

A bus shuddered by along Dawson Street. In the distance, those not attending to the speaker's words could hear chanting and catcalling from demonstrators outside the government buildings in Kildare Street.

Eilish Grace looked away from those before her and

rummaged about with her notes as though in search of something. She might have intended the comments for her own ears alone, so softly did she speak.

—Not shy, like we are anyway. Of the past. An odd thing, you might say, to want to rid yourself of the past. To throw out everything. Clearing out the house, of course, we seem to have gone a bit too far ourselves. Not only have we thrown out the bath-tub and the baby, but we seem to have thrown out all of the piping along with it. If you will forgive the extended metaphor. And what are we left with? Hmm? Catherine Connaughton's words on her incarceration are upsetting enough, even at this great remove:

'We all thought we would die when the fever came on some of the women. Me and this Agnes girl ... we would huddle in the corner of our cells at night. In case we'd maybe catch something off of the women there.'

The red-haired girl at the far end of the room shifted in her seat. Eilish Grace wondered whether she had an audience at all. Poor Catherine Connaughton, alone among the women in the jail. The loneliness of it. Poor soul. And what did become of her, really? Perhaps she did live to be released. And perhaps the McMorrow fellow and his friends were jailed for their part in the murder of Deveney. I could have checked that up, if I'd really wanted to. But I didn't want to. Did I? Maybe she went on to rear a family of her own. And maybe they too had children of their own. Did I pass some of her descendants on the roads around Crossmaglen the other week? Who knows, Whisht, woman! You're being stared at. What a fine head of red hair you have down there, love. Like Catherine Connaughton's?

—Of course, employing bailiffs to watch the land in order to keep local people from grazing their cattle on it, was common practice. With little alternative work about, many took the opportunity to earn their pittance this way, while ever mindful of the eyes of the Ribbonmen. Some compromised by allowing tenants to graze their cattle secretly by night. Doubtless, there were landowners who, for one reason or another, tended to turn a blind eye to this custom. The unfortunate Deveney, who met his death at the hands of the chastisers led by McMorrow, must have neglected to fulfil his obligations in some quarter. Violence is still a factor in everyday life in that part of the world, although we seem to have a reluctance down here to entertain the matter at all in our speculations.

One of the double doors at the end of the room was opened. A latecomer stole in meekly and a woman's hand closed the door again. The man nodded towards the podium. He set his umbrella in the cast-iron stand near the door. Eilish Grace paused a moment to watch the stranger. She did not think she recognised the thinning grey hair or the skin drawn taut over the bony skull. Your gamp you can leave at the door and your fancy accent at the station, her own mother would have said. She smiled at the memory and the grey-haired man returned the smile. Now she felt able to look into her audience once more and to read whatever their faces might portray of dismay or indifference.

—I'm put in mind of something a visiting scholar from Denmark once said to me many years ago. During my time on the staff of the folklore department in UCD. You seem almost ashamed, he said, when anyone brings up the word 'Ireland' in conversation. 'Why is that now?' And well he might have asked. We have come a long way to have reached that sort of psychological impasse, I suppose. How have we learnt to hold ourselves in such contempt? you might ask. Or, you might not ask, of course. And you may believe, and perhaps you are right, that this sort of riddle is — legitimately speaking — without the provenance of a lecture such as mine. But I don't believe so. What did a man like Seán O'Neasáin of Cooley have that left him in no doubt as to his origins and his place in the order of things? I'm not altogether sure myself, I might add. Was it simply his rural background? Did it have to do with community or common identity? Or was it maybe, a function of a nationalism that was based more on love than hatred? Something we seem manifestly incapable of fostering on this island. Perhaps it's beyond us. Must it always be a choice between hatred and indifference? Must it be a simple choice between the hatred of the future and the murder of the past? Is there no middle course?

A man in the front row who had mentioned over coffee that he had come all the way from Belfast for the day, turned his gaze to the side-windows for consolation. She felt her resolve troubled now. There appeared to be little response in the faces of her jurors. And, she thought that she had lost the sequence of the typed sheets in front of her as well. She cast about the lectern for the page which would give her a fresh cue. The two priests near the door whispered to one another. A younger man beside them looked at the floor and played with a newspaper. Eilish Grace scoured her thoughts for a code her hearers might understand. But, she thought, the little warm words have been stolen from them by the nothingness. Love, hate, happiness, sadness. They have all been replaced. Emotions are not allowed. And no wakes either. Too uncouth. Silence stunned with mechanical noise. Images burning our eyes and blinding us. Are these our new wake games? Games we play to distract ourselves from pondering the imponderable. Instant tradition-building. Freedom sold in dollops to suit marketing strategies. Consumer freedoms. The whole of Europe riddled with the worm.

The new fascism. That was what the Italian called it, she remembered. The subtlety of the beast though. And if I tell them this now, they will laugh at me. Poor Eilish Grace. Fighting fog again. You cannot fight fog, of course. Cannot fight what you cannot see or touch. Not like an army or a church. Worse even than dictatorship by church or state. We are our own dictators now, of course. Because we welcome the beast inside the gates ourselves. Trinkets for the natives. In return for what? This is not life. All change, no stability. Loosed from the soil by the city, we lose ourselves. Loosed from ourselves by the new animism, we lose our souls and our past. Words of the Italian:

'I see nothing in their eyes.'

Better to worship trees and stones. And then, the seal of the prophecy, when the sun bursts and we lose the prospect of generations. But only women would feel that, of course. Only women feel. They are staring at you Eilish! Speak girl, or forever hold your whisht!

—Later accounts of the collector O'Neasáin reveal to us the consequences of the girl's misfortune in playing witness to the murder of Deveney. The young girl Catherine Connaughton, by her own estimation, spent the best part of a year in protective custody in Armagh Jail. When she was released, it was on the understanding that she would emigrate forthwith, for her own safety. Let us hear how this touching little tale is concluded in the words of Catherine Connaughton herself.

Red-haired girl down there ... I see you and you see me. I am ranting on a bit, perhaps. You are smiling, though none of the men are smiling, of course. It upsets them, you see, being hectored and haunted by a woman. An ageing *bean sí* in retreat. Will no-one listen to me only you? But you at least are listening, red-haired girl. Here it is then: a carefully told lie to cap my tale. And what is a lie, when reality now consists of a stream of electrons and their scintillations on a cathode tube? A tribute to a girl and a cow and a tale already twice told.

—So, I was to rest at home until the first day of July, when I would leave for the boat. Now, I was very put out about the whole idea and I scarcely ate a bite for weeks on end. And when the night before the big day arrived, sure I was down to skin and bone. And my poor mother and father, God be good to them, didn't they stay up all hours of the night with the neighbours and they debating and discussing the thing. And I had my little red shoes laid out at the foot of the bed and brooches for my hair. My father used to call me foxy on account of the mop of red hair I had in them days. In the heel of the hunt, it was my mother who had the last say. She said she would as well have me stay and take my chances with the McMorrow tribe as have me dying of fever on the passage over. I heard it all, you see. From the loft. For I was no weight at all and ill along with it. Well, that was that. I recovered quickly enough after that, but my father never let me next nor near the cattle again. And I would often wonder, when I'd be alone with myself like, what it might have been life over in Boston maybe. Or Chicago. And everyone in their best and the buggies and the great fine herds of cattle. Then I'd forget the notion as quick again and I'd say to myself — sure aren't you as well off where you are now, Catherine Connaughton? And all your own about you. And in the place you know best. And sure people is more important than anything else. Would you not agree, Mister Neason?

Eilish Grace gathered up her notes and forsook the lectern. As she stepped down from the podium, she was suddenly aware of her own frailty. The way old-age had of wagging its finger at you when it saw fit. By a dull ache in the bones on a damp morning or the tricks time played with a mind less vigilant with each day. There were smiles from her audience as they stood for lunch. A harmless benediction of benevolent nods and smiles. She had unsettled them so. That much was clear. Had she discovered a new interest in that particular area of research, they wondered? The paper had certainly provided plenty of food for thought, they concurred. And she certainly knew how to speak her mind too. But then, she always had. Eilish Grace smiled.

—I don't think you like us very much, Mrs Grace. Would that be a fair comment to make?

The stark tones of Dixon of Queen's cut through the comfortable chatter. They smiled at one another. Eilish Grace passed down through the room. She declined an offer to dine with John Dixon. There would be another day. She thanked him sincerely. Over the heads of the crowd, she noticed the red-haired woman disappearing through the doors of the seminar room. She was disappointed in a way, that the stranger had not tarried. By the double doors, Morton of UCD and Celsus Redmond of Maynooth stood attending one another. They turned to greet her as she passed.

—The best wine 'til last, Eilish.

In the reading-room, at the long table, a solitary man sat beneath the lamps. She watched the silent, unseeing figure and reminded herself softly of her own embassy. She would leave the books and the dry bones aside altogether. She would leave the lot. She passed the book-lined walls and made their way under the balcony into the hall. Among the wood and brass, under the sour portrait of Atkinson, McNulty of Trinity helped her into her coat.

—It's chilly enough, you know. Even with the bit of sun.

The porter opened the door for her and she passed out and down the steps, a solitary woman with a smile on her lips and a music-bag of leather under her arm. She paused before the Mansion House gates to button her coat and cocked her ear to the chanting coming from the direction of Kildare Street. What were they protesting about? Her eyes squinted in the cold, sharp light of a sun which was turning on its heavenly axis to thrash the shadows along Dawson Street. She made her way home along the same route she had taken that morning. Crossing over Rath-mines Bridge, she decided that she would buy cold meats for lunch. That would be a nice treat. But was it right to eat meat on the eve of Good Friday? Not quite correct. But to scruple was not right either. She made her way up Leinster Road with the music-bag under her arm. In the sitting-room, she ate alone and, after a glass of dry sherry, lay down and slept for the afternoon.

EVE OF GOOD FRIDAY

In the house that night, Eilish Grace allowed herself no music. She would not have her feelings shrouded by the sensuous words of the Italian tenor. After the ceremonies of Good Friday however, she would be ready for the world again. She would follow the Stations of the Cross in Mount Argus and keep the black fast. On Easter Sunday, she would visit her grandchildren, as she had promised, and take them off for the day. Although she felt weary after the exertions of the morning, she coaxed herself into tidying the house. In the gathering gloom, she picked bluebells from the garden. She locked away the lecture notes in the davenport in Matthew Grace's study. They would not be needed again. She would find some pretext or other for avoiding publication. The case had been presented and they could think what they liked. She called herself to question once more on her way back down the stairs again. Had she really been living in a world as unreal as that of the collector O'Neasáin all along? Perhaps her criticism of things could, after all, be put down to the waywardness of a retired academic. She turned on the gas fire in the sitting-room against the chill of the April evening. In the mirror above the mantelpiece, she eyed herself uncertainly. No, it was true. All she had said. And more, which she had not said. Which she had not had the courage to say. She was sure of it now. What did it matter that her audience might have thought her obsessed with certain ideas? She had cried the cry of the corncrake before the harvesting machine. In the indifferent arena of the Academy, she had told of mankind being flushed out from the habitat of the heart. If even one had listened, then that was enough to justify her words.

She sorrowed at the world her grandchildren would inherit. For it was a world of images and abstractions. There would be neither name nor place there. A world of pinched souls in solitary apartment blocks. A world of night watchmen and tinny voices, whetted by static, crackling from receivers. No-one to kiss or curse or caress. There would be no family and no doors left unlocked. All would be one vast deserted global village. She must talk to her grandchildren more from now out. She must set seed in their minds. She must tell them that the past had been more than sickness and squalor and vacuous priests raging from pulpits.

Eilish Grace glanced at the photograph of her husband which stood on the mantelpiece. The picture had been taken just before his death, she recalled. In the Oval? Perhaps. Carson, the typesetter, looked out at her from the righthand corner of the photograph. The good thief. No, a photograph. Therefore the opposite side, of course. Therefore a bad thief. She smiled to herself. It all depended on perspective, of course. She shook her head slowly. It was incomprehensible to her that a spirit could be one moment and not be the next. It had nothing whatsoever to do with faith. Leaving down the magazine in her hand, she smiled at her own heretical wisdom. The heavy air of the room was making her drowsy. She felt her eyes drift from the words before her. She would retire and rise early the next morning. She stood up and settled the cushions on the settee. There was no harm in feeling that life had run its course. Was there? Now that she had given out her own message and that of Catherine Connaughton, what was there left for her to do?

She quenched the light in the sitting-room and bolted the kitchen door. The house was silent around her. There wasn't even the suggestion of a sound upon the air. Thinking that she had heard the rap of knuckles on the door, she crossed to the hall to enquire. But she opened the door to no-one for there was neither soul on her doorstep nor shade in the street. Who was she expecting to see there anyway? A red-haired girl with a smile on her lips? *The Fetch* come to call her home? She wondered once more at the ways of old age. On the return, she pulled the study door to once more. Then she continued up the stairs for the bedroom overlooking the spectral street. For, there was an easiness in Eilish Grace's heart now. No stir of apprehension to bully her thoughts. And she might lie down now with an easy mind. She might lie down in this fresh peace and dream now, before rising in the morning again and readying herself to meet her bridegroom once more, under a kinder sun and a softer sky.

The Women by the Window

THE FIRST THING about the nursing home was the cold, crafted face it presented to the world about. Although the sun had struggled through against the grey cloud of the late afternoon, the house itself still managed to stand aloof from that warmer season of the year. Crossing the tarmac stretch between the church and the home, she could see a face peering down at her from an upstairs window. She smiled for the stranger, wondering whether she might be looking at the woman she had come to interview. Catherine Hughes had not wanted the task at all. The hunger-strike in the Maze was to provide the backdrop to the whole venture. Against the impending dénouement of the fast and the steady decline of Sands, the central character in the cast, a request had come down from Features to interview the wife of the late John Devine, who had almost died on hunger-strike himself some sixty years before. What would the patriot of the Free State have thought of the present venture? Were there any obvious parallels to be drawn? The leading question would be framed, after the style of her editor, in a welter of sententious prose. Catherine Hughes glanced up at the windows once more. The face disappeared behind the curtains again. She read the inscription over the architrave.

ASYLUM FOR THE INFIRM 1891

It occurred to her that the woman with whom she would speak had been born but a fistful of years after the last cold stone had been set in the house. Nowadays however, the residents would not be drawn solely from the ranks of that particular congregation which had conspired to build the home. She thought to herself that she might try to avoid the issue of the North altogether. She would ask

Devine's widow about the position of women or her views on the Church. That would be safe enough. But not the North and not the present. Settling her skirt with her free hand, she entered the building. The lift with its trellis gate and the gloomy staircase to the right dominated the high-walled lobby. To the left, across the unpolished, parquet floor, a stairs descended to the basement, where the kitchen and the stores were situated. From the room opposite the reception desk, the sound of teacups and light chatter could be heard. A brass plate to the right of the door-jamb said:

DAY ROOM

She crossed to the reception desk. A small, squat, anxious- looking woman was busying herself with a dust-pan and broom. She was told to take a seat while the woman went to find someone in authority. Catherine Hughes was a slight woman, whose sure-footed bearing tendered the illusion of stature. She was firm with herself and knew patience. Her hair, bobbed in a pert pony-tail, was jet-black, as were her eyes. Strangers looking into those eyes read a resistance in them which did not tally with her smile. Silence seldom troubled her. Looking about her at the high walls of the lobby and the sombre cut of the furniture, she thought once more of the figure at the centre of the fast. The lank-haired man on the posters was dying quietly even as she sat there. It had been reported that blindness had set in and that the man's mind was wandering too. Renal failure would do the rest. It was disgusting. What had he come from? Housing estate to housing estate. Sectarian bitterness and social depriva-tion. That was the mix. It was easy to understand then. They were like the control rats in a laboratory experiment, driven to devouring one another by constant exposure to aggression and deprivation. Poor, sad Sands. And what about John Devine and his hunger-strike? Different social circumstances, of course. But, how could one be right and the other wrong? That was the danger: to get too close to the fire and to be lulled into sentimentality by the glow.

Better not to think at all. It was always possible to avoid these things if you really set your mind to it. But then, El Salvador and Nicaragua and Lebanon and South Africa? The thing in the North was intractable. One side was as bad as the other. There would never be an end to it. She smiled to herself as she murmured the same formulae of redemption which she had encountered in a thousand conversations. Primitives they were, all the same. The sort of squabbling over sectarian vanities which had not been seen in Europe since the religious wars of the Swiss. The whole thing was shameful. And what was the mess of pottage they had chosen to fight over? The right to fly one flag or another over the murky streets of Belfast or the dreary, provincial slum of Derry? The North was a nuisance. Poor, sad Sands. Dying for a dream born in a Belfast housing estate to the ramblings of a Presbyterian anarchist from the North and a Catholic fascist from the South.

The cleaning-woman appeared with the matron. Catherine was led upstairs into a small office which gave onto a nursery school to the rear of the house. One of the nurses' aides arrived in with a tea-tray. As they drank, the matron cautioned her again, as she had done earlier on the 'phone. There should be no mention of the house in the newspaper. Any such reference would surely be noticed and the board would get to hear of it. It was true, Catherine heard, that the house had always had its share of interesting characters with their tales to tell. She was told of one woman, a white Russian, who could remember the atrocities of the revolution with remarkable clarity. The matron inclined her head towards the window.

—And did you run into any trouble on the way here?

—No, not really. The guards are still outside the embassy though, and there's a lot of broken glass about.

—Isn't it hard to believe all the same, that it all happened around the corner, so to speak.

—It is, I suppose.

—Still, I don't know how you feel about the whole business, Miss Hughes ...

—Catherine ...

The matron stood up slowly and began clearing away the cups once again.

—Well, Catherine, I feel that he has brought it on himself. It is all self-inflicted. And, if you stop to think of it, there are thousands who die daily for want of a square meal. Who have no choice in the matter. Anyway, we shouldn't keep Mrs Devine waiting. I'm sure she knows you've arrived. She's like that, you know. Sees everything. Doesn't miss a thing. Well into her eighties too. We were going to give you the boardroom, but someone suggested that the nurses' room would be a lot warmer. So, there!

Catherine Hughes stood up and brushed the biscuit crumbs from her skirt. She was a daughter of the new city. Although her parents had migrated from Meath to Dublin when she was a child, she had no rural recall. Sometimes she wished that her parents had not paused in the capital city to take stock but that they had crossed to London instead. She had undergone a standard, suburban childhood of housing estates, shopping centres and mechanical noise. She had often thought that she might have felt happier among the maturer middle-classes of the cities of Kilkenny and Cork. There was something altogether disquieting about Dublin. It was an unlovely, social tapestry of too many noisome threads. Although she had associated herself in a limited way with the women's movement, she was uncomfortable with the dichotomy of thought which she found among its members. She felt no empathy with those who insisted upon a socialist dimension to the debate. When someone accused her at a party of being a typical product of late twentieth-century capitalism, she felt no wound nor did she see any call for countering the remark. She saw no need to pretend that she was other than she was. For this reason, those who found her notions of life repellent, still found great solace in her company.

When they entered the nurses' room, Mrs John Devine was already there. She was standing by an open window, looking out upon the children below in the nursery yard. She turned to greet them. Catherine noted the weak, tired eyes. It was the same face which had watched her as she approached the house. When the matron had set a chair for the older woman, she excused herself at once and left. It appeared as if the room had been tidied in haste. Cups, saucers and a milk-jug sat stacked in the sink. A discarded cloth lay by the draining-board and the face of the table still glistened with dampness. On the notice-board, below the shift roster, a clipping of a cartoon showing a bull and a toreador had been pinned. A nurse's forename had been appended to the drawing. The woman by the window took her seat. The tweed suit, choker and court shoes told the visitor that she had dressed for the day.

—Would you mind if I recorded the interview, Mrs Devine? It's a lot easier than making notes, you see.

—Ah, girl, I'm well past worrying about things like that.

—I just thought you might ...

—And don't worry your head about the matron either. She has her notions. It's in the blood, you know.

When the older woman spoke, her eyes bore the presumption of a smile in them. She talked, lightly at first, of the house and its inhabitants. From time to time, she paused to finger the satin choker at her throat or to settle her glasses. They turned easily, after a few moments, to talk of the days before the Rising. Of her childhood in Mayo. Of a father who travelled for the Congested Districts Board. Going from village to village with him. The poor of the west. Dampness and squalor. Dark-faced tinkers and TB-racked homes. Then, the Great War and the young men leaving again. And the plenty which was there to be seen, in the midst of poverty.

—There were some bad types, you see. There was a local landlord down at home in my parents' time. Hurson was his name. Barnaby Hurson. Lord Hurson. Well, anyway, the poor people used to say that when he died a badger leapt into his grave and dug its claws into the coffin-lid. Well, they beat it with their shovels and they tried everything to shift it. In the end, they had to bury Lord Hurson with the badger on his belly. The poor people used to say it was the devil coming back to claim his own. The poor people did.

Catherine lit a cigarette. The woman before her had settled into her stride now, and seemed not to need encouragement. She would give it time before drawing down to the particular, to the detail of John Devine's hunger-strike. It would probably be a sanctified event in the old woman's memory. It was scarcely possible that Mrs John Devine would criticise the actions of a dead husband and founder of the State. At any rate, she herself would not mention the Northern business to the old woman. It would be unkind. Had John Devine's hunger-strike been as gruesome as the one being played out that very hour? The body screaming for release, devouring itself for want of sustenance. The functions of life failing one by one. A man, a cadaver with the lustre scuffed from his eyes by hunger, crying pitifully to himself in a cell smeared with his own excrement. Was John Devine's hunger-strike no more dignified than this? The rationalising of history was a curious process, Catherine Hughes felt. The way the mind of a Lukacs might set particular circumstance against a general philosophical backdrop and extrapolate from there. Did that mean, then, that the present fast would be set in some sort of sanitising retrospect in fifty years' time by both winners and losers? It was all simply a matter of perspective then and there could be no objective viewpoint upon the thing at all. Therefore, there could be no onus upon her to take a stance upon the matter. She recalled the accounts she read of the negotiations between the Republicans and the clergy during the hunger-strike of John Devine. Why had he agreed to call off the fast and who had persuaded him to do so? She scolded herself quietly for not having mugged up the contemporary accounts before presenting herself before the man's widow. She turned back to Mrs Devine.

The fine, frail voice was momentarily lost against the sound of a child greeting its mother in the yard below the window. The woman spoke on, of the times before the Rising. Of the tail-end of the Women's Land League and the Volunteers with their wooden guns marching up and down the streets of a small town. She spoke of Carson's army and of a German band which had appeared in the town a few years in succession. Had that been before or after the war? She wasn't altogether certain now. Just that there had been great speculation that the Germans were charting out the whole of east Galway for some future invasion. Pipes and drums. Someone had gone to the bother of dressing the grave in the town-square again. Some maintained that the grave contained the remains of an unknown rebel, while others had it from their own that it held nothing more than the bones of a local law-breaker killed many years before in a raid on a landlord's house. Memory railed against memory and no one voice prevailed. Old stories, which had lain fallow for years, rose up again, ripe for the telling. The clamour seemed to be breaking out in small patches all over the country. Around that time, her father decided that she should be sent up to medical school in Dublin. After the great Lock-out. Under-nourished children and maintenance women. A tram into lectures each day in Cecilia Street. Before Catherine could draw the woman to speak of her late husband however, six o'clock had sounded across the canal from the home.

When the bells died away and the old woman had told her Angelus, she stood up slowly and suggested that they take a break below in the day-room among the other residents. On the way to the lift, they paused to greet another woman in her room. Two nurses, one pushing a trolley, came out of the lift. Catherine scarcely caught their muted words.

—I see Mrs McCreesh is back with us again.

—You never can tell.

—And how is she?

—Oh, she's only alright, you know.

—Is she supposed to be changed?

—The night shift will see to that. Around nine or thereabouts.

The house appeared to be settling down for the evening. They entered the day room almost unnoticed. It was as though the whole house had gathered at the bidding of the screen in the corner of the room. The evening news was in progress. There were images: a still of a smiling, long-haired youth. Then, another image of crowds passing by barricades, jeering at guards in riot gear. A flag burning on the road in front of the embassy. Voices shouting in the background. Taunt songs. A nurse, standing by the writing-table, nodded her head in bewilderment. Two domestics, who had slipped up from the kitchens, chatted together in the middle of the floor, aloof from the gathering. The smaller of the two, her face lined and dry, turned to her companion.

—How is he lasting this long at all?

—They had right to let them chaps out long ago. That's what I think, anyway.

—And why doesn't what's-his-name do something about it?

—Sure, what can he do? That one listens to no-one only herself.

When the news was over, Catherine sat with Mrs Devine in the company of the other women. The matron, from the doorway, told them that tea would be left into the nurses' room for them, but that there was no great rush. The domestics disappeared back to the kitchens once again. Catherine was introduced to each woman in turn. About the room, those objects which betokened the nature of the house, caught her vagrant gaze. The walls, which were hung with framed motifs and watchwords and the dark, sensible furniture. A plastic, kidney bowl, left aside absent-mindedly on a window-sill. When she turned back to the faces around her, the women drew her gently into their conversation. They spoke of their families, of the cold snap of the previous few days and of the 'flu which had carried off one of their number not a week before. Without intending to, the visitor gave an open account of herself. She could feel herself being tugged this way and that, by the sharp queries of the woman she had come to interview. And what part of Meath were her parents from exactly? And university too. Surely there couldn't be much call for philosophy in a journalist's job? And, she lived in an apartment. They must be terribly expensive in that part of the city. But there must be some man? Somewhere? And her hair! Wasn't that a lovely style, all the same? They say that the old fashions always come back, of course. What did she think of all that terrible business up in the North? All those young men dying for nothing. Where would it all end? Catherine Hughes turned to catch the eye of the woman who had thrown the question. Mrs John Devine smiled a guileless smile.

—There's no end to it really, I suppose.

The women nodded to one another silently or passed polite comment as the moment of her answers demanded. A woman with a newspaper folded on her lap winked at Catherine.

—Listen girl, I could write a book about my life. The stories I could tell you. A book, I could write!

—Only it wouldn't be fit to be published, Mrs McAlwee.

On the crest of their laughter, a man peeped into the room. Their eyes fell upon him and he smiled across the floor at them. Catherine Hughes noted how awkward the man presented, in a room heavy with women. Mrs Devine was standing at her shoulder now.

—That's one of Nurse O'Hara's admirers. You know, the little, red-headed waneen. He's great with her.

There were two nurses in the room when they returned. Both women stood up as soon as they entered and rinsed their cups quickly before departing. They set to talking once more. The older woman was lighter in her touch now. She seemed less taken with the tone of what she said and more with the substance. She talked of first encountering her husband at a political meeting in Wynn's Hotel. Her husband was a tall man, quietly spoken and sincere. He had recently graduated in chemistry. She recalled for the visitor, how he had walked her from Abbey Street to the Pillar. She remembered her uncle's hard words on her return to the house in Drumcondra and how he had barred her from attending any more political meetings.

—Ah, but he was good-natured behind it all. He used to say to me when I'd be off to a *céilí* or one thing or another,

'Off to your savage entertainments. Off to shake your apple trees.' He wouldn't hear of me having anything to do with politics at all. Lynch them all, he'd say.

Then the Cumann na mBan meetings she had attended. She spoke of something, which she felt unable to name, which had always held her back from close involvement in anything. Perhaps, she thought, it had something to do with her own background or personal fears. Or, yet again, her inability to trust wholeheartedly in the words of those around her. She told of her brother being sent over from the west to recuperate from TB. Of nursing Jim into his lonely grave during the very days of the Rising. His face blanched by the callous illness within. There was a time when the family believed that he would regain his health again, for had he not rallied just before the previous Christmas? She had scarcely noticed the trauma of Easter week for the misery of watching her brother sink under his burden. He was buried out in Glasnevin, her parents grieving that their son must lie under the alien soil of Dublin. Then, she herself falling ill under the strain, neglecting her studies and finally returning home to the west and the family.

—And there to greet me on the dresser was a pile of letters from John Devine. He hadn't been seen or heard of since Good Friday. They used to call him the Scarlet Pimpernel, because they could never lay hands on him. Have you ever heard that said? About my John?

—I've read that, alright.

—And, do you mind my saying something?

—Not at all ...

—Isn't purple an odd sort of a colour for a young girl to be wearing?

—Is it?

—Sure, you're not an old widow woman like myself yet. And did you knit that yourself, do you mind my asking?

—I did. From a pattern.

—Well, you have a pair of hands on you so. I can see that.

A short while later, the matron looked in to introduce

the staff nurse who would be taking over the night shift. All along the corridor now, Catherine could hear fresh voices greeting the patients. A small, cheerful nurse appeared in with a tray, telling Catherine that she need only call if she wanted assistance. The old woman sipped her tea with an unsteady hand, her darkened eyes straining against the fading light of the sky and the starkness of the striplights over their heads. Mrs John Devine began to talk of her husband once more. She spoke of his involvement in the troubles after the Rising and of their subsequent marriage. There was the house in Rathgar, owned by a close relative of John Devine, into which they had moved. A large, many-roomed building which housed three generations in comfortable isolation from one another. Her husband's lectureship in the university. How he had sidled out of politics before the war of the brothers came upon the country. The reputation John Devine gained for being openly critical of Church involvement in the affairs of the new state. The older woman stretched out her hand to the younger woman.

—John Devine could be as crooked as two left feet, so he could. You see, we had a soft enough time of it up in the house in Rathgar. We were well looked after. I was still involved in what was left of the co-operative movement. AE and all that. There was real revolution! There was danger! Changing flags doesn't matter a damn and John Devine came to understand that too eventually. What good did it all do some unfortunate fellow down on the docks? And he coming home to a damp house and hungry children? And his wife then, and she giving birth every year? A lot of silly old men. That's what the bishops were. And not too many of them lads ever wiped a baby's bottom. Or got up at all hours of the night to tend a sick child, let me tell you.

—Your husband was very critical of the Church throughout his life, wasn't he?

—How do you mean?

—Well, I've read of one particular incident which took place during the Rising. He said that it turned him against the Church more than anything else. He mentioned it in an interview he gave, just before he died.

—Ah, yes. I have you now. Well ...

Voices could be heard along the corridor. A nurse, giving directions, was calling two other voices to follow her. Men's voices. Mrs Devine suggested that one of the residents who had fallen ill the previous night was being removed to hospital for a second time. It was probably pneumonia, she felt. They could hear one of the ambulance men joking about the barricades in Ballsbridge. An elderly woman's voice called out from one of the rooms. The nurse was heard retreating down the corridor again. They marked the heavier tread of the men as they made for the lift with their patient. Then, quiet along the corridor once more and darkness settling in around the windows of the rest room. The older woman cast about as Catherine lit a cigarette. She smiled.

—Between yourself and myself, Catherine allannah ...

—I'm sorry?

—I said, girl, just between the two of us ...

—Yes ... go on ...

The older woman paused a moment, unsure as to whether or not she should continue. She watched as her cup was filled again, tapping her fingers lightly upon the table to signal impatience. When the hum of the tape-recorder had ceased, she began to speak.

—That story, Catherine, is all my eye. If there was one thing John Devine could do well and that was tell a good yarn. Oh, I saw him do it a hundred times to get himself out of a fix. Not really lying, though. Twisting the truth a bit. I suppose the story you mean is the one about the chap who was shot in the raid on the Broadstone? Doherty, I think it was. Is that the one you mean?

—Yes, I think so. During Easter week itself.

—And how my poor John, God be good to him, carried this unfortunate fellow up to the PP's house and how the priest refused to give the man extreme unction. Would that be the bones of it?

—More or less.

—And then, this Doherty chap and he dying out on the road like a dog. Well and aren't you the innocent girl all the same! If you don't mind my saying so. Ah no, dear, John Devine was a lot deeper than that now. The truth is, that he hated them — yes, he hated them — for what he felt they did to the people when the Free State was set up. The way they made stukawns of the people. He used to say, 'Let them bring their canon law and their informed consciences down to the Iveagh Market and see how much they get for them there.' He felt, you see, that we had pampered them for too long. He used to say, when he'd have a few drinks in him, 'We got rid of the crown, lads, but we should have gotten rid of the crozier along with it.' Ah, no. He only made up that bit of a story about the Broadstone and the priest. Maybe it was to hide the real bitterness. I don't know, to tell you the God's honest. But, you see, people can understand a bit of a story. But, if you start explaining things to them, it can get very complicated altogether. That's why you have parables. And sure, doesn't everyone like a good yarn?

Catherine Hughes considered quietly, the distance between a tale told and the shadow it might throw in the re-telling. She had been sent along to tease an opinion from the wife of a dead patriot. And now the woman sat before her. Not simply the shade of some querulous dissenter from the past but a deviant by her own lights. And where were all the women after the hullabaloo of revolution had died down? Where were the names and faces of those who had stood alongside the men?

—I suppose we all went off to have our babies. And then, of course, it was frowned upon to be involved in politics after independence. We were only in the way.

The tawdriness of the whole business touched the visitor now. How the gilt of revolution gave way so quickly to the commonplaces of everyday living. They were laughing together now, the younger woman coughing as she stubbed out her cigarette. The stooped woman in the tweed suit threw up her hands in delight. Then, there followed a lull. A gentle, untroubled silence. And now the woman was taking up the thread of her own life again, as though she had completely cast aside the notion she had been following just a few moments earlier. She told of the house in Rathgar, of her two children and her husband's work in the university. There was her own involvement in the language movement, which she dismissed as a form of sublimation. She spoke of a brief career, later on in life, as a medical librarian. The names of the day, of doctors and surgeons came to her lips. She mentioned her husband's memoirs, which were initially rejected by publishers because of their overt criticism of both Church and State. Then, the lampooning which had taken place when they were finally published. And the smug cartoon in the *Dublin Opinion*, which upset her husband so much.

—Let him go off to England with himself, if he's so fond of it, they said. That's always the answer if you're not in step with them here. Pack your bags. Running down his Church and country, they said. Oh, the knives were out. But John Devine was a tough old stick. He threw it right back in their faces. In the university too. They were twice as ignorant down there. Beggars on horseback. Our own gentry. Also, because of where we lived at the time, of course.

There was a nurse at the door to tell Catherine Hughes that there was a 'phone-call. She excused herself and followed the woman down the corridor. There were glimpses of faces as she passed their doors. The old and the bedridden. She overheard an exchange between two nurses who were trying to change one of the patients. The teasing and the coaxing in their voices. The weakest voice went almost unheard against the banter. She took the call in the matron's office. Closing the heavy door after her, Catherine Hughes considered her own unexpected stay in hospital a few years previously following a traffic accident. The old woman in the bed opposite, sunk into senility. How she ranted away to herself, clawing at the air and calling for her own to be with her. A man's name she had intoned over and over again. Catherine recalled waking at some uneven hour of the morning, to see the woman's arms raised imploringly to the heavens. To hear her low, steady moans as she forfeited her last breath to the world. The starkness of the cry against the silence of the hour. The raised arms silhouetted against the weak light of the observation booth at the far end of the ward. The eeriness occasioned in the observer's mind by the simple overlap of a few biological functions. Low sugar levels and depressed respiration. That barren reach between the darkest hours and dawn, where the old die softly and snatch-squads strike at houses to drag heads of families from their beds. She turned the memory to heel as she lifted the receiver.

It was McDonnell, one of the sub-editors from Burgh Quay, confirming an appointment for the following day. It had all been arranged then. She would meet the group of wives and mothers of the hunger-strikers in Buswells Hotel in the early afternoon. Leaving the matron's room, she did not go directly back to the rest room, but made her way down the stairs instead. She nodded to the nightporter on the reception desk as she passed and wondered about the following day's assignment. The women she had to meet would be, for the most part, young, committed and emotionally involved with the problems of the present. She opened the car door and took out the fresh tape and the book. It would not be as easy to talk with them as it had been to talk with the old woman in the rest room. It was a simple enough matter to trade off her own impressions of the events of the early decades of the century against the memories of Mrs John Devine. There was little conflict there. Any unease was safely lodged in a past mercifully obscured by the firebreak of her mother's generation. Nor did the old woman take her every word as bait, which the women she must meet the following day would. Their eyes would be as clear as their tongues would be sharp. They would probably mention the editor by name, recall for her his political stance on the hunger-strike and try to inveigle her into seeing the affair after their own fashion. She glanced up at the lights of the home as she crossed the tarmac once again. She should not keep the old woman any longer. The novelty of the day's distraction might suddenly turn to fatigue. She buttoned up her cardigan, as she gained the steps, against the chill which had suddenly come upon the evening. With an enquiring smile, the porter detained her as she sought to pass. They spoke about the cold of the night and the woman waiting in the nurses' room.

—I was just saying to one of the nurses there, that I'm only after hearing on the radio that there's more trouble up at the British embassy. They think you-know-who might be on the way out.

—Is that so?

—And no harm either, that's what I say. A right bunch of latchicos, the whole lot of them. And coming down here then to draw the dole. Get away out of that!

She drew herself away discreetly from the conversation. She considered the reactions she had heard around the town. The jokes about the hunger-strike. Slimmer-of-the-month in the Maze. And another, to do with H-block soup-of-the-day. Salted water. And there was a third one. How did that go now? She didn't remember. A nurse passed, bearing a tray on which a single glass stood. A spoon jangled in the glass. That would be someone's nightcap. And how the whole business had changed since the early days of the troubles. Then, a Northern voice was a popular turn in a pub or at a party for its dark-humoured accounts of bombings and shootings. She recalled some do or other which she had been at a long time ago. A tall man entertaining the crowd with a song about Barney something's bakery truck and the saving of the Falls Road. And the Monday morning after the march in Derry when the thirteen had died. The school she had been sub-teaching in then. An up-ended soldier-doll transfixed to the noticeboard with a compass. Now, the sound of a Northern tongue caused people to turn their backs and keep to their own circles. A patient was being helped to the bathroom. Another woman called from her bed for a nurse. There was the sound of brittle music from a radio in a distant room. The long corridor was hung with an old person's smell. Life whittling away at itself on the night. Back in the rest room, she found Mrs Devine standing by the window as she had been earlier. She apologised for delaying, then readied the tape-recorder to conclude the interview. When the old woman had settled herself once more, she handed her the book she had brought as a present. Drained, unsteady hands received the gift. The younger woman inclined her head in anticipation of the kiss which was laid upon her right cheek.

—Well! Aren't you very good, now.

Catherine Hughes turned away from the woman. She thought of the smiling eyes of the features editor as he spoke to her of the proposed interview with Mrs John Devine. How the matter of John Devine's own hunger-strike after the War of Independence would give a contemporary bite to his widow's words. The rattling of a trolley along the corridor outside provided a moment's relief. They could hear laughter from one of the rooms. It was a nurse and one of the patients. The old woman was smiling, passing a packet of butterscotch to her. She insisted that Catherine take one and leave the cigarettes where they lay on the table. The younger woman stood up to stretch herself and turned for the window. Behind her, she could tell the voice taking up its tale once more, as though there had been no distraction. Mrs John Devine spoke of her two children growing up. Of the war years and duck eggs and John Devine's death. She talked on, of the years after the war and her own work on the TB and dip-theria schemes. She told of a night in the children's hospital and an infant brought in suffering from chronic malnutrition. Feeding the child with an eye-dropper. The pale-faced scourge of consumption disappearing from the countryside. And her son in London and her daughter back in the west at medicine. For a while, the woman at the window lost herself to the shrouded view without the room. To the silent, stone mass of the unpeopled church opposite and the bare face of the tarmac stretch between the two buildings. When she turned back to the table, the old woman was grinning at her, as though waiting to cap her tale with some quiet joke.

—And throw me into the County Home, with a lot of old chatterboxes and they all sitting around in their farting jackets and they going on about fadder dis and fadder dat. And whist drives once a fortnight. Ah, no, I said. You can damn well fork out! Well, I didn't really put it like that, of course. You have to be hard sometimes, though. Even with your own. You'll learn that too, when you have children of your own. But, the County Home? Not for me, dear. Not for Sarah-Jane Devine.

The old woman signalled with her eyes that the interview had been concluded. Arm-in-arm, they made their way back towards the ward. At each door, they halted to say goodnight. The house had settled itself down for sleep now. Not even the hissing of the radio in the matron's office could take from the easy silence all around. Back in her own ward once more, Mrs John Devine saluted the two women who shared the room with her. The first woman, frail and dim-sighted, faced in to the wall for sleep as soon as they entered. The other, a stout woman with a fresh smile, sat up in her bed and engaged them in conversation. Answering the assistance button, a nurse's aide appeared and, leaning over Mrs Devine in the armchair, took a whispered instruction. When she returned a few moments later, she bore a tray on which three glasses of sweetened whiskey stood. She glanced at the woman in the far bed before making off again. The three women talked for a while, their conversation punctuated erratically by the heavy, sighing sounds of the sleeping woman. They spoke of the home and the staff who worked there. The heavy woman sitting up in the bed declared her personal preference for the night-staff. She maintained that the younger women on the day shift did not appear to understand the problems that age brought quite as well as the more mature women who filled the night roster. Catherine noted that each bedside-locker seemed to bear its own array of favoured books and photographs. She marvelled at the realisation that the bric-a-brac acccumulated by women must contribute in some way to the dignity of each.

A sewing-basket studded with mother-of-pearl or a lace doily under a table-lamp. Catherine Hughes stood to leave. Mrs John Devine told her that she would ring for the nurse herself when she finished her glass and was ready to retire. She looked up at Catherine from the armchair and raised her arms to receive the embrace. When the younger woman bent low, she whispered in her ear.

—The other's just between the two of us, now. Isn't it? What I told you about my John?

The old woman blew a kiss to her as she retreated from the ward. Catherine Hughes made her way down the stairs. She considered the woman she had interviewed. The saccharine anarchy of her smile. How ordinary and pedestrian seemed the details of John Devine's life when told by a confidante. Behind the splash headlines of the hunger-strike in the Maze, similar mediocrities would be at play. A child to be fed by a forsaken wife; a mother and father sitting in silence wondering about the sanity of their son's actions. She felt uneasy about considering the families involved. It was dangerous to portray the proponents of the drama too sympathetically. Was she not giving in to the tendency to dehumanise the enemy then? But then, if she ignored the thing altogether, would that sort of emotional censorship not rebound on her? To sound doubt was to invite comparisons with the manipulators of the hunger-strike. She was vaguely aware of a certain unease now, with her stated indifference to the whole problem. The issue of women being overlooked was easier to tackle. The facts of John Devine's anti-clericalism were quite comprehensible. But she had not allowed the Northern nuisance to bother her in a long time. Why give in to it now?

At the reception desk, she was waylaid once more by the night-porter. He looked up from the evening paper as she passed, cautioning her against going out into the night with her cardigan undone.

—That's how people gets TB. Never mind what the doctors say. They don't know everything either.

He told her of the patient who had been brought to the

hospital earlier that evening. There was great talk too, that the first hunger-striker had died. It was just a rumour though. As she made her way down the stone steps, Catherine Hughes considered whether or not she would have a meal on the way home. She had eaten very little since morning. She could drop into somewhere in town. The old woman's eyes came to mind again. Her soft indifference to the present upset. And how many were there now who were refusing food? She tried to recall from the posters she had seen all about the city. There must be six or seven maybe, including the man whose name was on everybody's lips. As she started up the car, she thought of what the night-porter had told her. The glint of anticipation in his eyes. Perhaps the smiling long-haired man on the posters really had died that evening. While she had been in talking with the woman. There was always the North now, like a sour-faced joker in the pack. How was it someone had put it in an editorial recently? Like listening to a clubbed foot being dragged up and down a darkened corridor in the early hours. Waiting, always waiting, for the unseen figure to halt before your door and for the terrible knock which must follow. And that other joke. Now she remembered it. The puffy-faced fellow from Waterford in Accounts had told it to them. It was he who had borne the joke into the office. His finger scratching out the words on the air before their faces. It was something he had seen written on a toilet door in Trinity that morning.

—We'll never forget you, Jimmy Sands.

The subtler message of a weak heart on the messenger's skin and in his strained laughter. Walking out past the dark mass of the Protestant church, she decided that she would make for town after all. She parked her car in a side-street and made for a cheap restaurant on Grafton Street. There were few at the tables. She fancied that the crowd was staying out of the city centre on the heels of that sense of gloom and foreboding which had insinuated itself into the pubs and cafés over the previous week. Without enthusiasm she picked at the plate of cold meat before her. She watched those around her. She felt comfortable in their company. Restrained couples, with a cheerful sense of dress. She wished somehow, that she could convey her own sense of puzzlement to them or even ask about the latest news of the leader of the hunger-strikers. But it would seem as frivolous as asking for a football score. They would look askance at her and make her feel silly for concerning herself with the thing at all. She shouldn't allow herself to be drawn into thinking of the problem at all. That was the only solution. To ignore the whole business. On her way to the toilets, she noticed that a radio was raging in the kitchen. Had they been following the whole drama, step-by-step? The grill chef seemed to be too busy to ask and she could not bring herself to question the kitchen porter who was scouring the banburies of the dried sauces. Could they really be following the whole affair while everybody else ate, oblivious to the last hours of Sands? A shame-faced sense of excitement steeled her heart as she sat back at the table to finish her coffee. A group of youths with Northern accents passed up Grafton Street shouting slogans.

—Ra! Ra! Ra!

Some of the couples glanced towards the window inquisitively, before turning back to their conversations once more. Catherine Hughes eyed the kitchens once again. It seemed incredible to her, all of a sudden, that she could be sitting here while the whole world waited for the latest reports from the cages in the Maze. The kitchen staff alone seemed to be aware of the mood of the evening. On the spur of indignation, she crossed the floor to the service hatch and smiled at the bearded grill chef.

—Did you catch the ten o'clock news, by any chance?

The young man smiled back at her. No, they had not been listening at all. They had only been keeping the radio on to drown out the noise of an alarm which had been set off on the earlier shift. She felt foolish now. Was she the only one in the whole city who was following the affair? Out on Grafton Street again, she turned for the back streets which fed onto George's Street. She could hear shouting and the sound of breaking glass up by the Green.

The noise sobered her thoughts suddenly and she was left with a sense of unmerited fatigue. She must leave the city centre right away. That was very clear. Perhaps the Northern business was like the notion of women in the infant years of the State, she thought. It had simply been removed from the agenda. It was not to be given a rational forum anywhere. But she didn't really care now, for the terror in her heart had driven the confusion aside. She must leave the city right away. That was the most important thing. She could go home by Ringsend and the Coast Road and avoid Ballsbridge and the environs of the British embassy altogether. That was the best plan. For it was always possible to avoid these things if you really set your mind to it. She glanced in the mirror and, brushing a stray lock from her forehead, drove out onto Grafton Street. She marked at once the clanging of the alarm and was surprised that she had not noticed it earlier. The kitchen staff would be deaf to the alarm she knew, the signal baffled by the clamour of music on the radio. She hoped that she would see nothing or hear nothing upsetting on the way home. Above all else however, Catherine Hughes hoped to skirt by any street trouble which might attend the news that the first man on the fast had indeed died.